Emily and the Key
By Og Keep

Rock and Fire Press
Salinas, CA

Emily and the Key
© 2023 by Og Keep
All rights reserved.

ISBN:
978-1-949005-22-6 (print)
978-1-949005-23-3 (eBook)

For Phoebe, and Julia, and
Kimberly, and Kirk, and Belle,
each of whom inspired a part
of this story; for Grant, and for
Nehemiah, in hopes that they may live
in a permanent state of revival;

And for Grace, who challenged me
to refine the metaphor of the hospital.

The author also gratefully acknowledges
Chase Thompson, and Victor Robison,
Whose comments, advice, and encouragement
Helped to make this work possible.

Chapter One

THE CHILDREN, BLESS THEM, dashed through the foyer of the church, scrambling to find nooks and crannies for hiding places, as Emily slowly counted down from twenty.

Emily, with her head resting against her forearm, leaned on the wall, straining her ears to follow the retreating footsteps. One of her siblings had gone into the children's wing, and another might have slipped into the auditorium... but then she should have heard the heavy wooden doors creak.

Emily was just beginning to stretch out, the way that children do just before becoming teens. Her arms and legs had gotten ahead of the rest of her, and her body would need to catch up. She had a mop of curly brown hair that cascaded from her head, and she sometimes worried that it made her look like a cocker spaniel, but that, of course, was nonsense.

When she would say such a thing to her mother, her mother would immediately deny it. Her father would wink, and then say that Emily's mother was right: She definitely looked more like an untrimmed Pomeranian, and not at all like a cocker spaniel.

Mrs. Cannon would hiss at him, and strike him with a pillow if there were one nearby. Emily knew he was kidding, because Pomeranians tend to be blonde.

Across the auditorium, to the right of the platform, past the piano, and through a heavy door, there was a hallway leading to the offices. Here, in the main office, her parents, Luis and Lupe Cannon, sat with Pastor Walter Dunwittee and Deacon Mike.

Lupe was a woman just entering middle age. She was still pretty enough, but it was no longer quite so easy to maintain her weight. Still, she hadn't given up. Her skin was light, but had a hint of darker shading, as if she were southern European, perhaps.

Luis was a dignified man, who always wore a suit to church. He was somewhat round in shape, though he carried it well. He was not a large man, overall, but no one would ever think that he had missed a meal.

His mustache was a thin line along the bottom of his lip, giving just a bit of emphasis to his mouth. His features would likely be classed as Hispanic, though with his light skin he could have passed for an Italian or a Sicilian.

Deacon Mike had a last name, but no one could agree on how it was pronounced, so he usually just asked people to call him Mike. He generally struck those who were meeting him for the first time as a large teddy bear. He was not too overstuffed, but he was also not a thin man. In terms of age, he would best be described as vibrant but well-seasoned. His hair was salt-and-pepper, with still more pepper than salt.

Pastor Dunwittee was slightly more formal than the others. He usually liked to be called by his title. He was of average height, and perhaps a bit thin, though not lanky or gaunt. The normal expression on his face often led strangers to believe that he had gotten lost, or was highly perplexed, which sometimes led to total strangers pointing out exits or restrooms for no apparent reason.

His light brown hair was shaped in a buzz cut, lying perfectly flat across the top, and he shaved his face every day. His suit was casual, with a corduroy sports jacket and a cartoon-character tie. If he thought Mike and the other deacons would allow it, he'd have stopped wearing the tie long ago; still, the tie helped him to project an image: The solemn and wise pastor.

"I was baptized when I was thirteen," said Lupe, with great emphasis. "And Emily has just had her birthday."

"Has she made a profession of faith?" asked Mike.

"What difference does that make?" asked Luis. "We have been coming to this church for years. Do you mean to suggest that we are not Christians?"

"Mike," said Pastor Dunwittee, in a conciliatory tone, "We probably shouldn't get hung up on fine points of creeds and such. It's about the people, after all." He turned to Luis. "Of course we'll baptize her if that's what you want," he said. "But we don't want you to think she has to be baptized. All of our programs are always open to everyone."

"We want her to be baptized," said Luis, crossing his arms and leaning back in his chair.

"Then we will schedule a service." Dunwittee rose, and offered his hand across the desk. Luis stood up and shook hands with him. Lupe nodded politely and started out the door ahead of him.

Mike had been perched against a bookshelf, and stood straight as the Cannons left the room.

"I'm not comfortable with baptizing people just because they ask for it," said Mike. "It's meant to be believers' baptism – a thing for people to do, well, when they believe."

Dunwittee scowled. Mike's traditional approach had been a thorn in his side for the entire time he had been at Sardis Baptist Church. He really wanted to open the eyes of this congregation to the dynamic styles of faith that were available in today's world; to help them be their own authentic selves, and Deacon Mike was just an old anchor weighing him down.

"Didn't Jesus say that he wanted the church to be a hospital?" he asked. "We need to welcome people where they are. It's okay to be sick; that's what he told the Pharisees." He got up and walked out, without giving Mike a chance to reply.

"Actually, no," muttered Mike. "That's not what Jesus said at all. He said that it is the sick that need a doctor, and then He healed them."

Mike felt the same tension that Pastor Dunwittee felt, but in the opposite direction. It seemed to him that the church was growing cold, and losing its edge.

Of the many metaphors for a church, perhaps his favorite was of a military outpost, left to hold a forward position until the General returned with reinforcements. It sometimes seemed to Mike that the pastor was far too friendly with the enemy.

In fact, there were times when he cynically wondered if he and Dunwittee were even in the same army, on the same side. When he would think such a thing, he would ask Jesus to forgive him. Still, the thought gnawed at him.

He had considered leaving the church, and finding one in which the Spirit of God was at work; where the people, and particularly the pastor, did not quench the Spirit at every turn. But he found that he could not. It is extremely difficult to abandon a place that you have once called home, no matter how painful it has become to stay there. So he had never so much as visited another church.

He left the office, making sure that it locked behind him, and made his way through the auditorium. Pastor Dunwittee was already well down the side aisle, and quickly vanished into the foyer.

"Mr. Mike?" asked Emily, running up to him. "I found this in the children's wing. It was on that sort of shelf thing in the primary room."

He knew the architectural oddity in question, and calling it a shelf was as charitable as any other name. Mike suspected that it concealed conduits, or an air duct, or some other poorly-planned piece of the building's infrastructure.

It occurred to Mike to wonder how Emily had found it, since the top of the shelf was well above her height. But he was not about to ask.

"Thank you," he said, receiving the object that she handed to him. It was a small key, the sort that opens a door to a house, and it was stamped with the numbers 48745. Out of curiosity, he compared it to the key for the front doors of the church. It didn't match.

"Do you know what it goes to?" she asked.

"Not the slightest clue," he replied. "But I'll see if I can figure it out."

"Emily!" came a sharp shout from the foyer; clearly the Cannons were loaded and ready to go.

"Coming," she replied, as she darted down the aisle and out of the auditorium.

Mike was left, standing, with the key in hand. It was brass, and darkly tarnished; mostly blackened but with traces of a greenish stain.

It was not at all shiny, the way that keys become when they are used often. Even the teeth of the key had a deep patina, suggesting that it had been a long time since this key had seen usage.

A few thoughts passed through his mind. Perhaps it might be for the kitchen, so that the children's workers could find snacks for their pupils. Or it might fit the restrooms, in case some youngster locked himself in. He supposed that it might even be for the gate to the play area outside.

In any case, it would keep. He made his way to the foyer, and found that he was alone. The only car outside was his own. He made a detour to the children's wing, where he left the key on top of the duct.

It probably wasn't important. Well, it obviously wasn't important: It had been left on a shelf for so long that no one knew it was there. It had had time to tarnish.

Still, something about the odd key intrigued him. It was like a half-finished book; he was very curious to know how it would turn out.

Perhaps he would come early to the deacon's meeting next Wednesday, and see if he could find a matching lock. But for the moment, he set the alarm and locked the church behind him.

Chapter Two

THE BOOK WAS VERY old, and very worn. The leather cover might have been hand-made, though if so, it had been made to a very high standard.

Once there had been words embossed on the cover, imprinted with gilt letters, but most of these had been worn away. In particular, the words along the spine were worn in the center, where a palm had cupped it. The shape of fingers in the wear pattern on the back cover testified that the book had often been carried; it was someone's close companion.

Mike had seen Bibles with this sort of wear, but this was not a Bible. The pages within were plain yellowed paper, perhaps once cream-colored. The margins of the pages were foxed with a brownish hue, and a few were cracked at the edges. Many were dog-eared; a few were creased. One was torn, and a few were missing.

The words on the pages were written in the slightly-too-careful hand of a literate but uneducated writer, perhaps from the last century. There were no dates, and nothing to indicate ownership or authorship.

Mike had found the book – the journal, or notebook, or whatever it was – in a small obscure closet, behind the baptistry. He had never noticed the door at all until he went prowling about with Emily's key, looking for a likely lock. Only then had it caught his eye.

The closet was only about a foot deep, and featured exactly one shelf, and exactly one object: This book. Well, there had also been dust: Dust sufficient to convince Mike that no one had opened the door, nor read the book, for a very long time.

But aside from the book and dust, the closet was empty. There was nothing to give him any clue about the purpose of either the closet or the book within it.

Mike opened the book to a random page and began to read the first entry his eye fell upon.

Sunday. Again I preached to the dry bones, and again they did not move into a right relationship.

Seven long years I have prayed, every week searching for the reason I have been sent here. In my entire ministry, not one soul has been saved. The baptistry has been dry, and the congregation dwindling.

Son of Man, can these bones yet live? Thou knowest, O Sovereign Lord.

Mike felt a surprising kinship to the writer of these words. He, too, had struggled to keep the church afloat and had struggled with frustration at the apathy he perceived around him.

Mike closed the book. It was more than he could bear at that moment. He sat in silence, trying to have hope that the church might come back to life.

The office door opened, and another deacon let himself in. The newcomer, whose name was Martin, had one of those faces that seemed just odd enough to be very memorable.

His nose was slightly too large and slightly too round, and Mike sometimes felt the urge to pinch it and say "Honk!" Martin probably wouldn't have minded. He was about twenty years younger than Mike, and had been in the youth group when Mike was a leader.

"Just us, Mike?" asked Martin.

"Looks like it."

"Whatcha got there? A new Bible? Your old one wear out again?"

"No, this is someone's prayer journal, I guess. Found it in a closet behind the baptistry."

"Pastor coming tonight?"

"Beats me."

"Well, maybe we can be done quickly. There's a game on. Oklahoma - Texas. The annual Red River Showdown, you know?"

Mike looked at his watch. Ten past seven; this was likely it. The pastor was seldom later than this, if he were coming. He took a deep breath.

"Okay, so, no visitor cards to distribute. No prayer requests. Oh, uh, the Cannon girl, Emily, her parents want her to be baptized."

"Did we ever fix the baptistry from last time?"

"I believe that, yes, we did have that fixed," said Mike. "Bad breaker."

"Those poor people. Duncan, that was the name. I remember, because we really dunked 'em… in ice water." Martin chuckled at his own joke.

"Well, room temperature, you know, tap water. It wasn't actually freezing that week."

"According to them, it was straight out of the Bering Sea. Just needed a polar bear to make it complete. Haven't seen 'em since."

"I'll personally make sure it's working this time," said Mike, with a deep sigh. "We'll try not to make an icicle of the poor girl."

Martin glanced at his watch. "Anything else? Kickoff starts in twenty-five minutes."

"Don't let me keep you from the game," said Mike. He watched Martin disappear and thought to himself, *Thou knowest, O Sovereign Lord.*

He didn't want to leave. It didn't seem like the meeting should be done so quickly. It almost seemed irreverent not to stay for a little while longer. Maybe there was still a word to be heard from God.

He opened the prayer journal again, flipping forward a few pages from where he had read before.

Saturday, another day of preparation. Today I was reading from Paul's letter to the Philippians, chapter 4, and found this: "Not that I speak in respect of want: for I have learned, in whatsoever state I am, to be content."

As I prayed over this verse, I felt great peace and felt the Spirit speaking to my heart: I sent you to go and to preach; in that you have been faithful. I prayed that my ministry has born no fruit, and the Spirit reminded me: It is God who brings fruit, not me; not by own my efforts, nor by my will.

I struggled with why God had brought me to preach fruitlessly, and I was reminded of the weeping prophet, and then a verse came to mind, from 2 Cor. 12:9, "My grace is sufficient for thee: for my strength is made perfect in weakness."

Then I understood. I must surrender my weakness in order to live by his strength.

Mike thought for a moment. He had done many things for the church, to try to see it grow. But in the end, it was not Mike's job to make the church grow. It was only his job to be faithful, and to give room for the Spirit of God to work through him.

He smiled, and felt as if a great burden had lifted off of his shoulders. He bowed his head. *Forgive me, O Sovereign Lord, for my presumption.*

Chapter Three

PASTOR DUNWITTEE LET HIMSELF into the church office. He needed to prepare a sermon for the next day. For several months, he had been simply downloading the notes from whatever was preached at one of the mega-churches that week. To his dismay, one of the senior ladies had caught him at it – apparently she listened to sermons online before coming to church on Sunday Morning.

That puzzled Dunwittee. Surely just one long-winded sermon each week should be enough for any normal person. He wondered if she were some sort of notorious sinner, who needed a self-imposed penance each week.

Dunwittee would be so happy when the church finally got over the idea of sin, and could move on into showing people how to live well, and to let go of all their negativity. It was a shame that the church was so caught up in medieval self-blame.

He turned on the computer and waited for it to boot.

It was an old computer, donated decades before, when it was merely obsolete. It now qualified as an antique. There were only two profiles under which one might log on, and neither was the administrator.

As a general rule, Mike would log onto it under the profile called "Finance," and Dunwittee would log onto it under a profile for someone named Charles Harris, who had preferred the username "HarrisC." Since no one knew the actual administrator login, these profiles were as immutable as the immovable ladder of Jerusalem.

All the drives made noises in their turns, even the 5¼" floppy drive. There was a long delay, during which Dunwittee wondered if there would ever be a budget that might allow newer technology.

After a few minutes, the screen turned pale blue and said something about "NTLDR not found." Of course, today of all days, the antiquated machine would decide to quit working.

He looked around the office, and for the first time wished he had actually brought some sort of commentary or study guide to the office. It would have given him a source from which to crib notes.

There was some sort of a crude leather-bound book lying on a top shelf. He pulled it down and flipped it open to a random page.

Sunday. I preached to very great effect on 1 Cor. 15:17, If Christ be not raised, your faith is in vain; ye are yet in your sins.

On the one hand, the verse seemed very narrow, and not the broad approach that Dunwittee liked. Still, the writer said that he had preached to very great effect. It sounded like he could at least make a few points with the sermon, raise his approval rating, and possibly give Mike a little less to argue about.

He blew the dust off of the study Bible on the next shelf down, an enormous Bible his grandmother had foisted off onto him when he first became a preacher.

Corinthians would be towards the back, among the letters of Paul. He was tempted to use the table of contents, but felt that a pastor shouldn't need it.

At last he found it, and read the entire chapter. Verse nineteen stuck out, slapping him in the face as he read it:

If in this life only we have hope in Christ, we are of all men most miserable.

Well, that was typical of Paul, to be so narrow. How could he say something like that? Christianity was good for many things, and could still help people, even if the Christ-myth wasn't literally true.

Dunwittee had been to one of those seminaries that teach psychology in place of theology, and in which the professors were skeptics who saw the faith as a palliative to keep the masses happy. To speak of the Christ-myth did not give him even the slightest twinge of misgiving. If someone were to object to the phrase, he would smile indulgently and say, "Of course, that doesn't mean that it's not true."

But Dunwittee did not believe that the resurrection was literally true. And that was the crux of his problem, so to speak. The cross was a path to changing these people, and it was merely a tool. Not something to be taken literally. Goodness, no.

He looked back into the journal, to see if it offered anything to soften Paul's harsh dogmatism.

I stressed that the resurrection is the core and the foundation of our faith, and that without it, we could all find something better to do with our Sundays. I demanded that they confront the cross; that each one ask himself whether Christ was raised from the dead, and that they each align their lives accordingly.

Seven came forward to pray; two professed faith and asked to be baptized. Praise the Lord for His Holy Spirit.

Well, maybe he could make something of that, aligning your life with your faith, living like you believed in something. After all, to have faith, there must be an object of one's faith, and the Christ-myth was, at least, a noble lie: One which gave people a good reason to live as happy and moral people.

Alright, maybe he could preach this, without any irony, and allow people to use their belief in the myth to have real faith.

That is, of course, precisely the opposite of what the passage actually says, in the most emphatic of black letters. Dunwittee had learned in college, however, that what someone says is not nearly so important as how it is said, and that meaning is a matter of interpretation.

And thus Balaam, son of Beor, prepared his sermon.

Dunwittee arrived early the next morning. Mike was placing dusty old books on the seats in the auditorium, about one to every three chairs. Several tattered cardboard boxes littered the platform, and he appeared to be getting them from these boxes.

"Mike, what's going on?"

"The projector's broken. Might be a burned out bulb. I'll pick one up on Monday."

Dunwittee picked up a book. It was a hymnal, and apparently the 1956 edition at that. "You're not proposing that we sing from these?"

Mike shrugged. "Mrs. Henson found them in a closet behind the baptistry. And with the projector broken…"

The church did not have a music team, or a praise band, or anything else of the sort. Mike would have been perfectly happy singing with a praise band, and most of the congregation would have been fine with it, but they had none.

The normal practice was to sing along with words projected from online videos. It was a simple and effective way to have music in the service without musicians. But with the projector out of order, they were in a bind.

"It's this, or sing as best we recall the words," said Mike. "Your choice."

Dunwittee frowned. For Mike to say that it was his choice meant that he had no choice; he was compelled to go ahead with singing from the hymnals. One step forward, three steps backwards. He shrugged, and then was distracted by Efrem Cannon, who was chasing his older sister down the side aisle. It looked like Efrem had a sword over his head.

"Efrem!" said Dunwittee, bringing the lad to a stop. "Where are your parents?"

"They're in the fellowship hall, making coffee," said Emily, who had stopped a safe distance from Efrem.

Efrem was still a couple of years from stretching into his teen form, and so was shorter than Emily. His hair was close cropped to his head, but not so fine that he resembled a bottle brush. His hair laid flat, what little there was. His green eyes, when he was up to mischief, gleamed, as now – though perhaps that was a reflection from the shiny sword he held.

"Where did you get that sword?"

"It was in a closet behind the baptistry," said Efrem. "There were a bunch of them. It's super-sharp, feel it!"

Dunwittee simply could not believe his eyes and ears. Swords, just stuffed into closets, where passing children could find them? No, that had to be utter nonsense.

20

"Bring that to me. You kids are not to play in closets. You could hurt yourselves!" He took the sword from Efrem. The grip of the sword was warm; slightly too warm. The silver filigrees of the pommel seemed to burn his palm ever so slightly.

It was an ornate sword, and the product of careful craftsmanship. Even Dunwittee, who had no use for weapons of any kind, found it oddly beautiful. Silver and gold, or metals like them, danced together in the hilt. Amazingly fine engravings marked words too small for the pastor's eyes to read.

Jewels, tiny and sparkling, shimmered in the light. Down the blade, in gold plated onto silver, was a single word: Durandel. When held slightly to one side, the word changed to something in Greek, and then held the other way, to a Hebrew script. It was a work of great wonder, simply marvelous in every way.

Still, it was nothing for children to play with. He marched to the office with it, to lock it safely away. He set it down somewhere, immediately forgot where, and then forgot why he had come to the office.

The service, even with its limitations, went well. Mike led the congregation through four old hymns that seemed oddly familiar to the older folks, and a complete novelty to the younger ones. The children spent most of the service flipping through the hymnals and whispering about what odd old books they were.

Dunwittee spent most of the song service gritting his teeth at the archaic texts and their sentiments: *Sinners plunged beneath that flood lose all their guilty stains?* The barbaric thought of dipping someone in blood – in actual blood! to make him clean! Dunwittee shuddered at the thought.

Could my tears forever flow, could my zeal no respite show, all of this could not atone; Thou must save and Thou alone? That was exactly the sort of self-loathing and the narrow view of faith that Dunwittee was dedicated to stamping out!

Dunwittee supposed that it was fortunate that the Jacobian-Georgian English tended to hide the meanings of the words themselves. And the music, anyway, was only stage dressing. The sermon was the centerpiece, and he would be able to use the narrow nature of the hymns to illustrate Paul's narrow view of salvation.

At last the dreadful singing – acapella, off-key, and badly out of sync – finally came to an end. Mike stepped up to the pulpit and prayed.

"Lord God, give the pastor words to speak that come from You, and from You alone. Render him invisible, and let us see only You, and hear only Your message. In Jesus' Name we pray, Amen."

"Thank you, Mike, for that blessing," said Dunwittee, as he came to the pulpit, trying not to roll his eyes at the idea of a message being from God. And it was at that moment that the sermon went completely off the rails.

"Let us begin by standing for the reading of the Word," he declared, absolutely unintentionally. He had not intended to say that, and it was his practice never to give any special respect to the scriptures that he was reading. Too late now, the people were rising up.

"Our scripture today comes from first Corinthians 15, beginning in verse 14: *And if Christ be not raised, then is our preaching vain, and your faith is also vain.*"

He had intended to only read verse 17, so he was a bit surprised to find himself getting carried away and reading the entire passage, but at least Mike would stop pestering him about context.

"Let's be clear: We could all have found something more fun to do today!" he proclaimed. "But we are here, presumably because Jesus Christ rose from the dead. And if you are here for any other reason, then as Paul said, you are here in vain, and we are the most pitiful of creatures!"

Wait. They couldn't be the most pitiful of creatures if they had the kingdom of God within them. How was he going to cajole them into self-actualization if he was telling them to believe the narrow gospel?

Maybe he was having a stroke. Or a seizure of some kind. Maybe he was suffering a psychotic episode. He would excuse himself and step down from the pulpit; Mike would catch on and would end the service.

"Excuse me," he said, "If that steps on your toes. But you can't have it both ways. Either Christ is risen from the dead, and we need to live like it; or else His bones are rotting somewhere near Jerusalem, and we should all be home watching the football game.

"The writer of Hebrews tells us, in Hebrews 11:6, that without faith it is impossible to please God, for those who come to God must believe that He exists, and that He rewards those who seek Him."

Okay, clearly, excusing himself and walking down wasn't going to work. Maybe he could simply walk away. But though he willed his feet to move, they stayed firmly attached to the floor, as if glued there.

For a moment, he wondered if Mike had done something with magnets to anchor his shoes. But that was just silly. His feet had to move. Still, no matter how strongly he willed it, they remained planted.

"If Jesus rose from the dead, then He is the Sovereign Lord of creation, and He deserves our honor and our praise – our highest service. And if he did not, then we should leave right this moment.

"I don't see you crowding for the door. I have to take from that that you believe. If you want to come forward and speak to me, I will be here, and I'll ask Mike and Martin … I don't see Martin, so I'll ask Mike … to come and stand alongside me. Please bow your heads."

Now, at last, his feet would move, but not in the manner desired. Instead of a hasty retreat to the offices, they led him down front, before the pulpit, at the mouth of the center aisle.

Mike took a position on the far right, as discreetly as possible. He was absolutely shocked at what he had heard. In his memory, Dunwittee had never once given an altar call. And the sermon sounded like an actual evangelical sermon, calling the congregation to faith in Christ.

But Mike was at peace. He had surrendered it all to Jesus, and resolved to worry no more. He would follow the leadership of the Spirit and cease concerning himself with the details.

"Mr. Mike?" whispered Emily, who was suddenly standing in front of him. "I believe. What the pastor said. I believe that Jesus rose from the dead. What should I do? I mean, I want to please God, like he said."

Mike sank to one knee, and with great joy, ushered Emily into the family of God.

When the congregation had filed out, Mike found himself alone at the front of the church, immersed in bliss. How the angels must sing, that a sweet child had found her way!

With a grin that would not leave his face, he made his way to the office. Dunwittee was there, sitting behind the desk and taking his own pulse.

"Feeling okay?"

"I think I might be having a stroke."

"Your face looks okay, and your speech isn't slurred. Do your hands feel weak?"

"No, it's just – that sermon. I had no intention of saying any of that. It just spilled out."

"Got a little carried away?" Mike shrugged. "That's not actually a bad thing."

"Those were not my words."

"Well, they came out of your mouth, and honestly, it was one of your better sermons."

"I don't know where those words came from. I didn't – My sermon was nothing like that. I..." he shrugged, with a look on his face like someone who was completely baffled by what he had seen.

"Well, I did pray that you'd be inspired," said Mike. "I'm going to lock up the front. You can turn out the lights and lock the office when you go."

---

1. *Sinners plunged… stains* is a line from William Cowper's 1771 *There is a Fountain Filled with Blood.*

2. *Could my tears … Thou alone* is a passage from Augustus Toplady's 1776 *Rock of Ages, Cleft for Me.*

Chapter Four

MRS. HENSON WAS, IN theory, teaching piano to the Cannon children. Unfortunately, the large eighty-something widow had a tendency to nod off, and was at that moment sound asleep on the front row of the auditorium, near the piano, her snowy ringlets shaking slightly as she snored.

This left the Cannons loose, and they were diligently exploring the maze of rooms and stairs and passages behind the baptistry. It was inevitable that they would come to the locked closet, and they did.

"Wait," said Emily. "I think I know where we'll find the key." She dashed down the steps. Efrem and Alyssa waited patiently.

"On Sunday, this door was open, and I found a sword in there," said Efrem. "It was super sharp, and it was really fancy. With like jewels and stuff."

"Whatever," said Alyssa. She had no interest in swords and things like that. Still, she did have a very distinct curiosity about locked doors.

Alyssa was compact in size, slightly lighter than Emily in general coloring, and had straight brownish hair that swung around her shoulders. Her mother called it a page boy cut, though Alyssa sorely resented being called a boy. A tiny mole, hardly larger than a pencil point, marked her left eyelid. She was completely unaware of the mole, because when her eyes were open, it wasn't visible.

Emily was gone but a moment, and returned with the key in her hand. It was still deeply tarnished, but there was a bit of a shine at the edges, where the patina had been scraped away.

Alyssa took the key and opened the door. The closet was, as usual, almost empty. On the single shelf there was an odd little crown.

It seemed like something that might be worn by a woman, and the first word that popped into Emily's head was "Tiara." But a tiara is only a half-circle, and this crown went fully around the head.

Alyssa popped it over her brow, and it fell down onto her nose. Efrem giggled and Emily laughed.

"Obviously, it's not for children," said Emily.

"Let's put it on Old Mrs. Henson," said Efrem. Their eyes all lit up, and they darted down the stairs to where Mrs. Henson softly snored. Emily lifted the crown from Alyssa and gently set it over Mrs. Henson's curly white hair, where it rested nicely.

The children stepped back. The crown seemed to change the old woman. She seemed less wrinkled, and her hair seemed to take on a slight tint of blonde coloring.

"She's lovely," whispered Alyssa.

"It's like it made her younger," said Emily, quietly.

With a soft Hmmph! sound, Mrs. Henson snapped awake. "Oh, children," she said, in a quaky and feeble old-lady voice. "Where have you been?"

And then there came a sparkle to her eye. She drew a deep breath and smiled.

"All hail the power of Jesus' Name! Let angels prostrate fall! Bring forth the royal diadem and crown Him Lord of All!" she sang, in a powerful soprano that resonated throughout the room, bouncing off the high ceilings, and ringing from the corners. It seemed to Efrem that he had never heard music until that moment, and to Alyssa that it was like the choirs of angels on Bethlehem's plain. Emily's mouth fell open as she stared.

"Pardon me, children," said Mrs. Henson, her voice at once strong and vibrant. "I shouldn't be bursting into song, but I was simply filled with joy. Now, we were learning our scales. Efrem, take a seat and find middle C."

Efrem, unable to do anything else, seated himself on the bench and struck a note.

"No, child, move one octave to the left." She smiled. "Would you girls like to learn a song about the scales? I learned it when I was a teenager. It was from a movie."

She led them through the song, as Efrem hesitantly tapped out the scales behind them, and the Cannons senior arrived to find their girls struggling to match Mrs. Henson's melodious carol.

They stood for a moment, amazed, taken aback by the transformation in Mrs. Henson. She reached the end of a chorus and turned to see them in the aisle.

"Oh, are we done already?" She clucked her tongue. "We were just having such fun. Well, children, off you go. See you Sunday. Love you!"

The children, still slightly perplexed by the sudden transformation, made their way down the aisle, glancing back from time to time at Mrs. Henson, who now looked distinctly younger.

As they passed through the foyer, they heard her burst once more into song: *"Teach me some melodious sonnet, sung by flaming tongues above!"*

When the song finally came to an end, and the chorus ceased to echo through the chapel, Mrs. Henson reached up and found the diadem round her head.

"Oh, Lord God," she prayed, "I cast down my crown before Thee; Thou alone are worthy of glory."

She carried the beautiful diadem into the office and dropped it into the trash bin.

The janitor, Hiram Cheebly, did not find the diadem later, when he emptied the trash in the office. Hiram had one of those faces that seemed to fit in anywhere, and looked ever-so-slightly like someone that you knew. He was an older man, and the salt-and-pepper in his hair was now mostly salt.

He made his way through the church at a leisurely pace, picking up, dusting, cleaning, emptying, and polishing, as the need presented itself.

In the upstairs room behind the baptistry, he found a door he had never noticed before. There was a key in the lock. Out of curiosity, he opened the door, but the odd little closet was completely empty. He closed the door and removed the key.

As he made his way to the children's wing, where there was usually more than the usual amount of cleaning to be done, he noticed the key in his pocket. For lack of a better place, he put it on top of the shelf.

Pastor Dunwittee was having a very strong cup of chamomile tea, with an extra spoon of artificial sweetener, to try to help him relax.

Sunday's highly unusual sermon – well, if he had ever believed that a person might be possessed, it was after that frightening incident. Honestly, it was as if he didn't have control of his own body.

Mike had prayed that he would be invisible. Clearly, that was a metaphor. Still, maybe it was some sort of a curse – well, that was silly. Mike wasn't a witch-doctor, invoking spirits... Except perhaps the Holy Spirit. Did Mike put the Holy Spirit on him?

For a moment, he was angry, but a nagging thought kept tugging on his sleeve. In the Bible, people who were overtaken by the Holy Spirit did great works for God. So if he really had been overwhelmed by the Holy Spirit of God– that meant that the things he said were what the Spirit would have said.

And since the things he had said in the sermon were completely contrary to his entire philosophy of ministry, that meant that the sermon was completely right, and Dunwittee's ideas about God and about the church ... were ... wrong. Completely and utterly wrong.

It would mean that God was real, yet transcendent; a Being capable of changing physical things in a physical way. It would mean that Jesus actually died on a real cross and rose again from the dead. The Christ-myth would be a Christ-fact; not just a pretty story to inspire us, but the actual sacrifice of the Creator God to redeem mankind.

Dunwittee sat perfectly still for a moment, trying to absorb that idea. Then he shook his head. Obviously, that was the chamomile talking. He poured about half of his tea into the sink and replaced it with hot water, resulting in colored water that simply tasted slightly off.

Much better.

The next day, Dunwittee made his way to the room above the baptistry, and found the mysterious closet, but of course, it was locked. He tried to remember where

Mike had said that the girl found the key – was it on the shelf in the children's wing?

He returned with the key and tried to push it into the lock, but at first it didn't seem to be the right keyway. He studied it, rattled the doorknob, and then inserted the key, pushing it firmly into place. At last, it clicked nicely into position, and at last the doorknob turned.

On the single shelf, there stood a hurricane lantern, the kind that had been used in steam trains, a century or more ago. It was burning, and it filled the closet with blinding light. Dunwittee stared. There had been no light showing beneath the door, and no one had been here in the church for hours, at least.

He felt the door, and the shelf, and the wall behind the lantern; each was cool to the touch. There was no sign of the fire in the lantern, save the lantern itself. He carefully brushed the backs of his fingers against the glass globe, but it was actually cool.

Had someone lit a fire and left it unattended, locked in a closet? But that sparked a memory in his mind: A Bible verse about lighting a lantern and putting a basket over it. He remembered wondering, as a child, why that wouldn't set the basket on fire.

Well, however a burning lantern had gotten into the closet, he couldn't leave it there. He took the handle and lifted the lantern out of the closet. He had no idea how to extinguish a lamp like this, so he decided to take it to the office, where he could look it up on the internet.

Lamp in hand, he made his way down the stairs. He had to hold it high in order to see all the way to the bottom of the steps. It was at that moment that he noticed how dark the church had become, aside from the bright yellow glow cast off by the lantern.

Crossing the auditorium, he was struck by how very odd, how very ancient, how very numinous, it seemed. The church was built less than a century ago, and yet there seemed to be something unspeakably old in the very air. The room seemed oddly solemn and consecrated, set aside in some deep and mysterious way. He fancied that he could hear a faint chant of monks, off in the distance.

Motion near the vaulted ceiling caught his eye, and he held the lantern higher. A faint smoke, or a mist, seemed to rise into the highest peaks of the ceiling, and swirled there, as if the prayers of many generations had coalesced into a visible form. It seemed to thicken, as strand after strand of smoke rose into the rafters.

They seemed to have a scent: a scent of sweet spice and bitter despair, of joy, of incense, of fervor, and of anguish. Perhaps he heard them faintly; many voices, out of time and out of sync, but all united in a whispered melody, whose meter just escaped his rational mind.

And yet the hall was silent.

There was a Bible verse about the prayers of the saints, like incense smoke, rising from the altars of God. Could this be like that?

No. No, this was not happening. He was not seeing this. It was some fancy of his imagination, some delusion, some hypnotic suggestion brought on by being alone in a dark building.

He closed his eyes, and on reopening them, found himself inside a perfectly normal room, illuminated by perfectly ordinary electric fixtures, and holding a slightly odd but perfectly ordinary hurricane lamp. It was not lighted; it didn't even seem to have fuel in it. The wick was too short, anyway.

He'd had too much tea, obviously. He resolved to cut his chamomile dose even further, and to buy a different brand the next time.

It seemed clear to him what was going on. Someone was playing pranks, leaving things in that closet, and tricking people into opening the door. From there, the mind played tricks, making normal places and things seem oddly spiritual.

Hidden key.

A closet filled with odd objects: journals and swords; hymnals and lanterns. What nonsense. Utter rubbish.

He resolved to throw the key away, but for the life of him, he could not recall where he had left it.

1. *All hail… Lord of All!* is a line from Edward Perronet's 1779 *All Hail the Power of Jesus Name.*

2. *Teach me some … tongues above* is a passage from Robert Robinson's 1758 *Come, Thou Fount of Every Blessing.*

Chapter Five

LUIS FOUND THE KEY, right where Emily had described. The children and their silly talk over the dinner table, about finding things in a closet – A sharp sword, and a diadem – it was too much nonsense.

Children made stuff up; it's what children did, in Luis' mind. But if there was a place in the church with sharp objects and crazy old things that could get broken or stolen, Luis wanted to make sure that it was properly secured. For safety's sake.

The key was on the shelf. The door was right where the kids had said. And the key slid easily into the lock. The single shelf was almost bare, save only for a roll of undeveloped film.

It was the old style of film, from back before digital cameras. It was a thirty-six shot roll, and Luis strained his brain trying to remember a place that still developed that kind of film. At last, he settled on the old camera shop down on Main Street – if it was even still there!

He closed the door and took the film with him.

The following Tuesday, Martin Clark, the other deacon – that is, the other active deacon – walked into Dorman's Café and saw Luis sitting at the counter. Luis had finished his meal, and was looking at small papers. Martin took the seat next to him.

"Luis, fancy meeting you here."

"I come here for lunch every Tuesday and Wednesday," said Luis. "It's usually very quiet. And they have a really good cheeseburger."

"I hope I'm not interrupting anything."

Luis lifted his head from what he was doing. "I found an old roll of film at church. I got it developed – I have no idea what this is from." He handed the envelope of photos to Martin. "Mean anything to you?"

Martin's heart stopped.

The first photo leaped off the paper. It was taken at the chapel on the old campground, up at Pascal's Lake. There was a service going on, and a boy was kneeling at the altar, praying to receive Christ.

Martin still remembered that old chapel. Even now, sitting in the café, a strong scent of pine filled his nostrils. He could hear the band, a Christian-Punk group that had been a big deal in the 1990s. He could feel the carpet beneath his knees, and hear the words of the speaker: *Who has the Son has life, and who has not the Son has not life.*

He was the boy in the photo; the boy kneeling at the altar. His mind refused to accept it. What were the odds that someone would hand him a random photo, and that it would be of him?

Martin put down the pictures. He turned to Luis, hoping that his face did not look as pale as it felt. "Where did you get these pictures?"

"I told you," Luis replied. "In that old closet, at the church. I found a roll of film. I had it developed, just now. You wouldn't believe how hard it is to get a roll of film developed these days. It's like …"

He stopped talking because Martin wasn't listening. He was staring, slack-jawed, at a photo of three boys riding an oversized inner tube down a steep snowy hill.

"Well," said Luis, throwing a twenty onto the counter to cover his meal and the tip, "You find out what that's from, you let me know, okay?"

The waitress came around minutes later, and had to ask three times before she got Martin's attention and took his order.

Wednesday Night services were typically Dunwittee, Mike, and the Cannons. Health permitting, Mrs. Henson often made an appearance.

Tonight, Mrs. Henson, moving with a grace that belied her eighty-something age, was practically dancing down the aisle. She took a place near the front. Usually, it was to be better able to hear; tonight, it was to better express the joy in her heart.

Dunwittee moved towards the pulpit, intending to mutter a few words about loving one's neighbor, and also loving oneself. One's authentic self, the perfect human with the kingdom of God already within him or her, that is; that was who Dunwittee wanted them to simply love.

Mrs. Henson stopped him. "Pastor," she suddenly asked, projecting her voice loudly and clearly in a manner that startled everyone present, "Would you mind terribly if we were to begin with a song?"

He took a step back, which she took for assent, and in a moment she was at the rostrum, head held high, arm raised to signal the beat of the song.

"Sing with me," she instructed those present, "From the very first hymn in the hymnal: Holy, Holy, Holy."

Dunwittee and the Cannons looked around for hymnals, but Mike merely smiled serenely. The words of the hymn were tattooed onto his soul.

Mrs. Henson sang with fervor and feeling, hitting every note precisely, holding it for not one millisecond too long. Dunwittee muttered the lyrics under his breath, as best he recalled them, aghast at the words. *The eye of sinful man Thy glory may not see?* Come now, were we not all equal before God? How judgmental, to call someone "sinful man!" And *seraphim, falling down before Thee?* Why the emphasis on humility and self-immolation? No wonder the latest generations didn't like church.

The Cannons mumbled softly along with the words, occasionally pausing to shush one of the kids, who were busily elbowing each other and whispering about what the diadem had done to Mrs. Henson.

Mike simply opened his heart and worshipped God.

As the hymn drew to a close, Emily blurted out a request. "Could we sing *10,000 Reasons*?"

To everyone's surprise, except Mike's, Mrs. Henson not only knew the Matt Redman song, but was able to lead them in all three verses. Their voices hung together somewhat well, but Mrs. Henson was able to embroider small filigrees into the song in several places. On the third verse, Mike found himself shouting "Forevermore!" just before the chorus.

The door at the back opened slightly, and Mike glanced back to see Martin slip in. He took a place on the back row and didn't sing along. But when the music stopped, he raised his hand.

"Could I ask a prayer request?" he said, when all eyes turned towards him. "It's unspoken. Well, I, wait. No. Never m. Okay." He paused, to give his words a chance to coalesce.

He took a deep breath. "It's for Susan. My ex-wife. You all know her, well, Luis and Lupe, maybe not, but everyone else. I'm going to Big Bear to go talk to her. I called her the other day and she didn't hang up. So I'm gonna go, and we're gonna talk, and… Well, pray that the Lord softens her heart and gives me good words to say."

Lupe and Luis nodded.

Normally, at the mention of Big Bear, Mike would've made a joke about bearing with him, or the idea being unbearable, or something to do with furry animals. But he held back, for Martin's sake. It just wasn't the right time for it. So instead, he said a silent prayer that Susan would hear Martin's heart, and not his words.

Luis raised his hand as well. "I know we don't normally do this," he said, "But Mike, what you said a couple weeks ago, it got me thinking, you know, what does it mean that we're Christians, right? I mean, how are we so different? So could you all pray that God would speak to me, to, you know, show me what we're supposed to do? I mean, about living out the faith."

"Certainly," said Mrs. Henson. "Now, I've been having trouble with my hip – well, until last week, that is – and I'd appreciate your prayers on that, as well. Brother Mike, would you lead us in prayer?"

Mike nodded, and prayed for Susan to receive Martin graciously, and that perhaps there might be, if not a full reconciliation, at least a repair of the relationship. He asked God to give Luis guidance, and to heal Mrs. Henson's hip, either by His own hand or by that of the doctors. He offered a psalm of thanksgiving, and closed in Jesus' Name.

In the silence that followed, Martin spoke again.

"Could we sing that song that goes, *When I survey the Wondrous Cross?*"

"We can," said Mrs. Henson, "And we will."

Dunwittee sat on the second row, wondering how the service had gotten so badly away from him. He listened in anguish as the small ensemble sang of pouring contempt on all their pride. Christianity was meant to be affirming, and life-giving. This song was just so utterly antithetical to what he was hoping to achieve.

After the service, Luis cornered Dunwittee before he could disappear into the office.

"Listen, Pastor," Luis said, "When are we going to be doing the baptism for my Emily? I need to know so we can get the whole family here, and have like a party, to celebrate. This needs to be a big deal, so I need to get it on the calendar."

"Ah," said Dunwittee, who, truth be told, had forgotten the proposed event the moment the meeting had ended. "Well, we're almost into December, with, you know, Advent and all that. So it's hard to say when… Maybe after the first of the year?"

"I don't know if Lupe will want to wait that long," said Luis, with reproof in his voice. "The sooner the better, you know."

"Well, we will need to make some preparations," said Dunwittee, as he struggled to remember what sorts of things a baptism required. Weren't there robes involved? Some sort of oil? Incense? No, that was the liturgical style… No worry; he'd simply look it up on the internet.

"What preparations?" snapped Luis. "Come on! Just fill up the baptistry and dunk her in the water. It's not like it's brain surgery."

"Would you want her baptized on Christmas Day?" said Dunwittee, with a hint of sarcasm. "We could do that if you really want."

"Yes," said Luis. "Yes, that would be perfect. My parents will be in town for Christmas, and Lupe's parents just live over in Smyrna, so they could easily come over for the ceremony. It can be a Christmas dinner and a Christening, all at once."

Luis walked away, leaving Dunwittee standing alone, slightly bewildered. Mike walked over to him and put a large hand on his shoulder. "Feeling okay? Not another seizure or anything?"

"No, but, listen, Mike, things are getting out of control around here."

"That might be a good thing. But what now?"

"Luis and Lupe want to baptize Emily on Christmas Day. But that's not the problem."

"Aside from Easter, I can't think of a better day for it. And, by the way, I tested the baptistry heater. It works now. We can have the water hot with as little as three hours advance notice."

"Fine, fine, whatever. But this trend in the music – listen, can't we get the music back to something modern? Something written within our lifetimes?"

"I'm sure we can," said Mike.

The smile on his face made Dunwittee suspect that when he did, Dunwittee still wouldn't be happy with it. He longed for some of the modern worship songs that had catchy tunes and words that, if analyzed carefully, meant very little or nothing at all. Songs about vague spirituality, that was what he wanted. Something about angels gathering, or something vague like that.

"Whatever you do with the music, you've got to get Mrs. Henson onboard with it. This can't go on. She can't suddenly take over the Wednesday Night service and turn it into a prayer meeting."

"Heavens, no," said Mike, in a flat tone. "A prayer meeting. Oh, the horror."

"I'm serious," said Dunwittee. He was tempted to give Mike a stern rebuke, but he honestly didn't dare. "We can't have her undermining our leadership like that."

"Maybe she should be a leader."

"The senile–" Dunwittee stopped and surveyed the area around them, to make sure Mrs. Henson wasn't within earshot. "There is no way we can put that senile old bat into leadership. She's stuck in 1950."

"You say that like it's a bad thing," said Mike, with a smile. "But I'll see what I can do."

---

1. *The eye of sinful man Thy glory may not see* and *seraphim, falling down before Thee* are lines from Reginald Heber's 1826 *Holy, Holy, Holy.*

2. *All of my gain I count as loss, and pour contempt on all my pride* is a passage from Isaac Watts' 1707 *When I Survey the Wondrous Cross.*

Chapter Six

MRS. HENSON DREAMED OF the key, and the closet. In the closet were ten lamps; the ancient style with the wick in a narrow spout, resembling for all the world a modern gravy boat. One, out of the ten, was lighted, and a feeble flame barely escaped it, giving a dimly fluttering light to the rest of the closet.

This cannot be permitted, she thought. She closed the closet door, and returned a moment later. She had found five jars of oil, which she placed alongside the lamps. Four of the lamps sputtered and lighted themselves, joining the fifth, which now burned brightly.

The other five remained as they were: Cold, and dark, and oil-free.

Well, she thought, *That's a little more like it. At least five can be ready for the Bridegroom when He comes.*

The sermon on being inclusive was just not going well. Dunwittee had read the first four pages without even thinking about them. He was concentrating hardest on putting the right emphasis into his words.

The church should be like a hospital. That was his theme, and as a starting point, he had read the parable of the good Samaritan, which was as close to a hospital scene as he could find in the New Testament. He would go on to say that we shouldn't exclude anyone, even sinners who refused to repent, in order to be like Jesus in His inclusion of the marginalized. Or, that was Dunwittee's plan.

He was on page five when he heard himself saying, "One does not go to a hospital in order to show everyone the depth of one's sickness. One goes to a hospital to be treated. And just as one does not go into a hospital and refuse treatment, one must not come to the church and refuse repentance."

Was that actually in his notes? It sounded much narrower than he had meant it. It was supposed to be broad, and about accepting people who were different, and not locking people out of the church for not seeing things our way. But as he heard it coming from his mouth, his sermon was sounding narrow and exclusive.

He paused and took a sip of water from a glass on the pulpit. It was intended to give him a moment to check his notes, and to see if he was saying the right words. Sure enough, he was exactly on point. The words on the page, however, were completely different from the words he had written there.

"If you have come today so that others can see how boldly you defy God's standards, then you have come in vain," he said. Those were the words on the page; words he could not possibly have written. Wait... had he said them out loud?

"Amen," said Deacon Mike, a bit too loudly.

Yes, he had said them out loud. And more words like those were pouring out of his mouth.

"We are all sinners." He cringed at the word, but couldn't stop himself. His hand refused to clamp itself over his lips, however hard he wished it.

"But that's not an excuse to continue to sin. In Romans 6:1, and in Romans 6:15, Paul asks if we should continue in sin. Each time, he answers his own question: Let it never be!"

It was happening again. There was nothing he could do. He would have to simply let the words run their course. And so he kept preaching, all the while praying that the sermon would be over soon.

Martin was also praying that the sermon would be over soon, but not because it was out of sync with his own thoughts. It was too much in sync, and was burning holes in his soul.

Martin had long felt that his loose style of worship, being just Christian enough, without being too Christian, and carefully avoiding any sort of creed or dividing line, was good enough. He usually enjoyed Pastor Dunwittee's sermons, mainly because they were toothless and unlikely to cut deeply. Today, not so.

The pictures from camp had shaken him. The photo in which he had been giving his life to Christ, and committing himself to follow Jesus – that had been a bolt of lightning. But the next photo, of him and Susan sharing an ice cream sundae on the return trip, had been a bigger jolt by far.

They were too young, and they should both have counted the cost. They were so wrong for each other. He knew that now. Still, it had seemed so perfect, back then. And a few years later, when they had turned eighteen, they had married. Too soon, too young.

Oh, to be able to tell himself, his younger self – but that wasn't possible. It soon became apparent that they were headed in different directions, and momentum tore them apart. The marriage lasted less than a year.

In that moment, that single hour when they had both realized that they were better apart, he had lost not merely his wife, but his best friend, as well. He looked, now, at the picture of them sharing ice cream.

He wished he had seen it then: that they had no common foundation. He had given his life to God; she had not. He had decided – at least in that moment; in the old pine chapel at Youth camp – to make the Gospel his purpose and his goal. But that was not their common goal, and their life together could not be founded on rock and on sand at the same time.

When he lost her, his approach to the Christian life became loose and full of meaningless rituals. His theology became inclusive and broad. He dared not be narrow, because that would exclude her and her sinful lifestyle. It would be like excluding his right hand, or his right eye.

It was at that very moment, as Martin's thoughts rested on Susan being like his right eye, that Dunwittee, trying with all his will not to, recited Matthew 5:29.

"Now if your right eye is causing you to sin, tear it out and throw it away from you; for it is better for you to lose one of the parts of your body, than for your whole body to be thrown into hell."

Dunwittee winced inwardly as he saw Martin blanch at the thought. Clearly, he had struck a nerve.

To Martin, the idea of casting Susan away in order to save himself was unthinkable. Another verse came to Martin's mind; a verse about having something to settle with one's brother, and leaving the temple to go and settle it. He would not cast her away; he would instead go and redeem her. He got up and hurried out the door.

"You did ask for more modern music," said Mike, when Dunwittee chided him after the service.

"The Newsboys' *Not Ashamed?* Honestly?" Dunwittee shook his head.

"I guess that the 90s were a while ago," said Mike.

"It's not that, it's the lyrics. They're so…"

"Openly and unapologetically evangelical?"

"Ah. I see what you're trying to do. And that version of *Holy, Holy, Holy?* Where did that come from?"

"It was a Christian punk band called Undercover. I guess it was around 1983 or so."

"Look, why can't we do some of those soothing songs like I hear on Christian radio? The ones that are kind of inspirational, but still not, you know."

"Not confrontational?"

"Yes. Exactly."

"Because after all," said Mike, with heavy sarcasm, "We wouldn't want anyone to change how he lives as a result of our service."

"No, we *do* want people to change how they live. We want them to love themselves and to accept other people just as they are, without any judgment. I don't think you understand what I'm trying to do here."

Mike shrugged. "Maybe not. But it wouldn't be the first time."

Dunwittee turned without comment and marched out towards the office. As Mike turned back around, Luis was there.

"Mike," he said, sharply, "I was never aware that Martin had been divorced."

"Well, it's not something one normally shouts from rooftops," said Mike. "But it is true."

"The Bible says that a deacon cannot be divorced."

"Actually, it says that a church leader must be the husband of one wife."

"He is not the husband of his wife."

"I'm a single man, myself," said Mike. "Widowed now for a dozen years. Does that exclude me as well?"

"No, but… Okay, see… Yeah, I don't know what the Bible says about it, but I know deacons can't be divorced."

"I can tell you for certain that Martin is not the husband of more than one wife. But if you'd like, we can take it up at the next deacons' meeting."

"That's – you and Martin?"

"Unless the pastor shows up."

"Perhaps I should take it up with the pastor."

"I believe he's in the office," said Mike, as he moved towards the light switches.

Hiram came in later to clean the church, as he did most Sunday afternoons. He was worried, because he had used the last of the hand soap filling the dispensers in the ladies' room, and he was fairly certain that the dispenser in the men's room was empty.

Usually, the church secretary was very good about reordering supplies, but he was afraid that perhaps she had forgotten. When he looked on the shelf, his suspicions were confirmed. There was no soap.

Unless, perhaps, she had left it somewhere new. Hiram retrieved the key from the shelf in the children's wing and took it to the closet. As he opened the door, he immediately spotted a gallon jug of pink hand soap.

Just what he needed.

On Tuesday, Dunwittee came to the office to sketch out his sermon plans for December. Clearly, not planning his sermons was leading him to ramble, resulting in the last few sermons that had missed the mark. Or at least, that was what he believed, or what he had rationalized in order to keep from thinking that he was losing his mind.

The problem had to be psychological; that's what all of his training had taught him. Therefore the answer would also be psychological, namely, to take control of his conscious mind and to plan every word in advance. He would practice each sermon out loud – perhaps he should even record himself. Yes, brilliant idea. He could catch the points where his mind wandered, and direct it back onto the main topic.

He began with the advent wreath. Each candle would lead him to a sermon topic. The prophets' candle – well, he would talk about the confusion concerning prophecies, such as whether Isaiah 7:14 really meant that Jesus would be born of a virgin.

For the Bethlehem candle, he'd talk about the so-called census, and that would lead him to the Herodian problem and the Quirinian problem with dating Jesus' birth. Of course, he knew that scholars had so-called solutions to these problems, but his point would be on the importance of believing in something, even if it were completely wrong.

The shepherds' candle would be a good place to ask if there were really shepherds sleeping out in fields in December. Even in the Holy Land, that would be very cold. He could mention that the shepherds were just a literary theme so that the gospel-writers could call Jesus a shepherd when He began His ministry.

The Mary candle … well, there were so many things he could say about Mary. Yes, that would give him four weeks of material, until he got to the Christmas Day sermon. Then he could tie it all together, how the Christ-myth gives us hope that we can change and become accepting of ourselves and of others.

It did not, for one moment, occur to him that he was teaching heresy that was dangerous both to the souls of the congregation, and to his own soul as well. He was perfectly willing to say virtually anything, so long as it led people to affirm themselves and to love themselves.

His eye fell on the leather prayer journal, where Mike had left it, on the top shelf. On an impulse he flipped it open to a random page and read a few words.

Wednesday Night. I reproved a young man for his false doctrine, pointing out to him the James 3:11 rebuke: "My brethren, be not many masters, knowing that we shall receive the greater condemnation." I cautioned him in the name of God to refrain from additions to God's word, lest the Spirit of God rebuke him harshly.

Well, that was very narrow. And based on how badly things had gone when he last took advice from this journal, he probably shouldn't look at it again. He threw the journal back onto the shelf where Mike had left it.

While Dunwittee prepared heresy to preach in place of the clear and simple gospel, Mike sat at his kitchen table and read the Christmas story from Luke's gospel.

He loved Luke, with the clear touchstones to secular history: The census of Quirinius, for example, who we knew, from archaeological evidence, had been made a duumvir of Syria – a joint-ruler, or co-governor – in about 6 BC, thus resolving the dating gap between Herod and Quirinius.

Or Luke's clear reference in Luke 3 to the fifteenth year of Tiberius, when Jesus was about thirty years old; fourteen to fifteen years before Tiberius would be in the reigns of both Herod and Quirinius.

Mike found the Word compelling him to pray, and so he opened both his heart and his mouth.

"Lord God, Maker of heaven and earth, I praise you for Your Son. I praise you for Your Spirit, which even now moves among us. Lord, do not cease moving among us, I pray, until your word has watered the earth, and your Spirit has renewed our hearts to a right relationship with Thee. And above all, Lord, please do not cease putting words into the mouth of Pastor Dunwittee."

He rose from his prayers and found a song in his heart, and for the rest of the day, he caught himself bursting into song, reciting a joyful refrain.

Chapter Seven

IT WAS YET FOUR Sundays until Christmas, when Dunwittee planned to drop the bomb that the Christ-myth might not literally be true, and still might guide us to be moral and just. Today's goal was to undermine the idea of Jesus being predicted in the Bible.

For a moment, doubt bloomed in his mind. What if he were wrong, and God – not merely the idea of an all-powerful lawgiver, but a real transcendent Being – had really and truly condensed Himself into a helpless baby in order to speak as human to human with humans?

No, that was just too silly for words. He turned his eye to his notes, rehearsing them in his mind, planning the emphasis he would place on all the key words.

As he sat in the office and read carefully through the blatant heresy he had prepared, Mike sat in the back of the church, where he had queued up several songs to show on the projector. Preparations having been made, he sat on the last row and prayed.

He did not, like Niebuhr, believe that prayer changes the one who prays; he instead had the simple audacity to think that in prayer he held the ear of God Himself, and could make his needs known to the power that holds the universe together. Time and again, responses to his simple prayers had led him to confirm this belief.

Emily came in and seated herself beside him.

"Mr. Mike?" she whispered. "Are you awake?"

He opened his eyes and smiled. "Yes, of course."

"In our Bible lesson, we read about Isaiah 7:14, and how it was about a child named Immanuel. But that's not Jesus' name. Were there two babies?"

Mike smiled. It pleased him, deeply, to explain such things. Not because he enjoyed the sound of his own voice, but rather because he loved the thought of helping someone along the path to the Truth Incarnate, namely Jesus of Nazareth.

"Yes, there actually were two babies," he said. "This prophecy was fulfilled twice. In the days of King Ahaz, there was a baby born to symbolize the fall of Assyria, whom Ahaz feared. And at the same time, it is a symbol of Jesus' coming, and that He would not just be called Immanuel, but would really, truly, be God-with-us, the God of the universe condensed into a human baby."

"Oh," said Emily. "So the first baby, Immanuel, was also himself a prophecy of Jesus."

"Throughout all the Jewish scriptures," said Mike, "There are people who are a little bit like Jesus, to give us hints of what Jesus would be like. So that we would know Him when He came."

"Why didn't the Bible just say it in plain words?"

Mike thought about it for a moment. It was a very profound question, and he was proud of young Emily for thinking so deeply.

"I'll tell you what I think," said Mike. "I think that if people had known that God was coming, they would have put on their best clothes and they would have kept Him among the kings and the high priests.

"But Jesus wasn't just for the high and mighty. He was also here to save the simple folks – people like you and me. And they never would have let us near Him, if they had known who He really was."

Emily smiled. "Thanks, Mister Mike!" she said, as she darted off to join her siblings, who were making themselves cocoa in the fellowship hall.

Mike stood up, and noticed a small group of strangers in the foyer. He hurried over to greet them.

Lupe Cannon, as her husband helped their children to make cocoa for themselves and coffee for the congregation, thought of her marriage. She loved the children, of course, and Luis was always supportive. But it was not like it had been, in the olden days. Not like when they were first married.

Sometimes she wondered if he really still loved her. And to be honest, she didn't always feel like she was in love with him. Love was supposed to be magical, and about kisses and flowers. Not about dirty laundry and sick children and listening to him rattle on about his work.

Jesus would surely understand if she were to leave him; Jesus was all-loving. He would want her life to be joyful and fulfilling. Of course she would wait until after Emily was baptized. She would never disrupt her little girl's special day. But after that... Who knows?

At that moment, a stray thought came to her, as stray thoughts often will, and she remembered hearing the children talking about a key and a closet. Perhaps she should see what all the fuss was about. On an impulse, she left the fellowship hall, where her children were making noise and her husband was rebuking them for being messy.

The closet was right where they had said, and the key was already in the door. It was not dark and tarnished, like they had said. She could see where many fingers had worn the surface smooth and clean.

The closet was almost empty, and it took a moment for her to see the single small object on the shelf. It was a small golden ring, and once she saw it, she wondered how she had overlooked it. It gleamed with light, as if a special beam of sunshine somehow penetrated through to this tiny little closet.

The ring was a single continuous band of brightness in her hand. There was a single small card, dazzling white, where the ring had lain. It was gilt-edged, and a square of gilt, with delicate filigrees, outlined its margins. She held it up to read it:

The King of Glory, Almighty God
Is pleased to announce
The wedding feast of His Unique Only Son:
Jesus of Nazareth, the Christ
The honor of your presence is requested.

R.S.V.P. at once.

She chuckled. Well, that was a unique tract, and very clever, but how had this humble church been able to afford such an expensive printing? Hopefully, they hadn't given out rings like this one; the cost would have been simply insane.

She lifted the ring to examine it closely, and found writing inside of it. She read the inscription and began to feel light-headed. It was her initials, and the date of her wedding to Luis:

Only two people – no, three, counting the jeweler – knew the inscription inside her ring. It had not been off of her finger since that day. And yet this ring was a perfect copy of the one on her finger.

She dropped the ring from her hand, and heard it roll across the floor. Who could know what was on her ring? Who but God alone?

And that fact – that this ring was here, with the secret inscription within – it was clearly a sign, and meant that her marriage was not merely a matter between her and Luis; God Himself was a party in the matter.

She hurried down the stairs, across the auditorium, and out to the fellowship hall. Luis was surprised when she threw her arms around him, but he had learned not to question her impulses. He simply hugged her back.

Once the service started, Dunwittee endured the singing. He had to admit, on a purely objective level, that it wasn't as bad as it had been. Most of the people were now on the right key, and a few actually followed the tempo and the melody.

There were some new voices: He was startled to find visitors in the back on the right. That was a surprise, but it was bound to happen, just randomly, from time to time.

The part of the music that irked him was, once again, the lyrics. One of the songs Mike had chosen – in cahoots with Mrs. Henson, no doubt – was the Charlie Peacock song, *In the Light.*

He remembered how he had despised the song when DC Talk had recorded it in the 90s: All the emphasis on sin as a sickness, and on Jesus as the only cure. It was exactly antithetical to what he wanted to teach them: That they, the people, were the cure to their own problems, if only they would stop condemning themselves and start to affirm their own goodness.

Well, at least he would have the sermon to turn things around. Who knows, perhaps the new people would see what he was trying to do, and would become new allies in his struggle.

Mrs. Henson took the pulpit and began reading prophecies, as Efrem Cannon went forward and lit a candle on the advent wreath. She began with Genesis 3:15, then Micah 5:2, Isaiah 7:14, and Isaiah 9:2 through 6.

As she spoke of people living in darkness seeing a great light, she gestured to the prophecy candle, and then made her way back to her seat.

Well, at least Isaiah 7:14 would give him a jumping-off place for his sermon on the non-prophecy. He took the pulpit with confidence.

"Mrs. Henson," he said, "You missed one of my favorites, from Numbers 24:17, *I see him, but not now; I behold him, but not near. A star will come out of Jacob; a scepter will rise out of Israel.*"

He smiled at the congregation, but inwardly, his heart sank. It was happening again, and he couldn't prevent it. It was actually getting worse. It was not a favorite verse: he didn't remember ever seeing that verse at all before this moment.

"Those words do not come from a saint of God, and that is part of why I find them profound. They come from a seer named Balaam, son of Beor, whom the Israelites soundly cursed. He is the one Jesus refers to in Revelation 2:14, when He is reproving the church at Pergamum: Balaam, who taught Balak to cast a stumbling-block before the Israelites.

"This enemy of Israel, when called upon to curse the Israelites, could not stop blessing them, instead. In fact, here, he calls out the coming of Jesus, which was not to happen until some thirteen or fourteen hundred years later. The Words of God cannot be confined; no earthly plot can hold them back."

Dunwittee's eyes widened in terror as he realized at last what he was experiencing. God was speaking through him in the same way that God had chosen to speak through Balaam's donkey, and through Balaam himself.

And yet, even with this obvious sign, Balaam did not repent, thought Dunwittee. *I'm Balaam's Donkey! Oh, Lord, what have I done?*

"And yet, even with this obvious sign, Balaam did not repent," said Dunwittee. This puzzled him: Were his words finally matching his thoughts, or had his thoughts aligned with his words? He glanced at his notes. He was supposed to say something about the Hebrew word *Alma* simply meaning "Young woman."

"There is another prophecy that I love," he said, clearly missing the *Alma* point. "Back in the dark days of the Babylonian captivity, a prophet highly favored by God, Daniel, gave us another great prophecy.

"In Daniel 9:25, the angel Gabriel says this to Daniel: *So you are to know and understand that from the issuing of a decree to restore and rebuild Jerusalem, until Messiah the Prince, there will be seven weeks and sixty-two weeks.*"

Dunwittee paused. He was definitely not in control, and it was starting to occur to him that he wasn't supposed to be. This was a clear and obvious sign; one he had best heed.

"If you are wondering why God was not more explicit in the Bible about where and when the Messiah would come, Mrs. Henson, earlier, read from Micah 5:2, that Jesus would be born at Bethlehem, and here Daniel tells us when: 483 years after Cyrus allowed Jerusalem to be rebuilt!

"We have the time and we have the place: Even history itself declares the unstoppable Word of God. Now let me ask: Do you, personally, know that Word, the Word who became flesh and dwelt among us? If you do not, please see one of the deacons after the service."

He closed his Bible and nodded to Mike, who came forward to close the service with a benedictory prayer.

Chapter Eight

AS SOON AS THE congregation had departed, and Dunwittee was alone in the church, he ran to the children's wing to find the key. It was now polished and gleaming, and it fit smoothly into the lock.

On the single shelf, there sat a Bible.

It was a fairly poor example of a Bible, as Bibles go. It was a mass printing edition of an inexpensive trade format, and it was in exceptionally poor condition. The faux-leather cover was cracked in several places, and torn along one edge of the spine, where it flopped loose. On the other side, it was held by threads.

Dunwittee knew, before he opened it, that the type face on the left-hand pages would be slightly darker than on the right, and that the red letters, indicating the words of Christ, would be slightly misaligned with the black ink. He knew that the pages would be onion-skin thin, and almost transparent, and the font face so small that it could only be read in good light.

Had he found it on his shelf, knowing nothing else about it, he would have thrown it away. Most likely anyone would; it was that tattered. Holy Bible or not, it looked ready for the trash bin. But He knew better; this Bible was oddly familiar to him.

On the outer cover, the owner's name had once been embossed in gilt letters. Someone, many years after the printing, had rewritten the faded letters with a yellow fabric marker. The name was clearly legible, and it took only a glance to see that this Bible had once belonged to his father.

He opened it to a random page, and found Daniel 9:25 underlined with a red pencil. There, his father's unschooled handwriting had marked the margin: *only 483 years until Jesus!*

Dunwittee sank to the floor, his back against the wall, the Bible loose in his hand. He thought of his father, a simple ranch-hand from Texas, and how, in spite of his hard work, he had been tireless in talking about Jesus.

Dunwittee remembered rolling his eyes at the gospel his father had taught. He remembered spending countless church services coloring in the Os in the bulletin to stave off boredom. His father, the lay-preacher, who could have slept in on Sundays after six long days of hard work, had instead gathered the children, Sunday after Sunday, and brought them, or rather, dragged them, to church.

His father had owned very little on this earth. He said it was because he was a stranger in the land, saving instead for a heavenly home. Dunwittee had always believed it was because he didn't know enough to make any real money, and hoped in heaven for relief from hard times on earth.

His father's meager savings had sent him to Bible college – his father's choice, and not his own, of course – and then to a seminary. Dunwittee would have rather studied rock guitar and racecars, but that would have broken the old man's heart.

And if his father could see him now, would he be proud of his oldest son? Was this the legacy that the godly ranch-hand had sacrificed and saved to produce? No, it obviously was not.

In the dark little room next to the closet, Dunwittee sat alone and cried.

Luis returned to the church building just in time to see Dunwittee leaving. It was just as well. Lupe had been talking about the closet, and Luis didn't have the slightest idea what she was talking about. All he had found in there was a roll of film. It had cost him nearly twenty dollars to find out what was on it.

This time, when he opened the door, he found a small scroll, tied with a red ribbon. As he untied the ribbon, the scroll opened. Old English letters, the very fancy ones used in diplomas and in old Bibles, jumped off the page at him.

The first letter, an O, was the size of three lines, and had been decorated with ornate images of birds and vines, in fancy colors, with gilt edges around them. He read the words:

> *Once upon a time —*
> *Say, for example,*
> *Friday at about six —*
> *Would you go with me*
> *To dinner and a movie?*
>
> *Yours Happily Ever After,*
> *Luis.*
>
> *p.s., I have arranged a babysitter.*

Now, there was a clever idea. It had been a long while since he and Lupe had been out for a date night. Old Mrs. Henson seemed to take kindly to the children... Perhaps she might accommodate them.

He re-tied the ribbon, making a bow, and carefully adjusted the lengths of the ends. It did not, even for one moment, occur to him to wonder how the scroll had gotten into the closet, or how his name had come to be at the bottom of it. He only knew that he had to go home and give it to Lupe at once.

As he let himself out of the church, he called Mrs. Henson to see if she were available Friday Night.

Warren Dunwittee, of Nocona, Texas, for whom it was already late in the afternoon, had a sudden stray thought about his older brother. Warren was a hard man, who had spent much of his life outdoors. His face had that peculiar reddish-brown tone that comes from sun and wind, applied over a long time. When he relaxed his face, the creases near his eyes opened into tiny canyons, telling the world that he squinted more often than not.

Walter, Warren's brother, lived out in the small town of Sardis, California. Warren often felt that it had been a grave mistake for his father to send Walter to that Bible college and seminary out west, but that was part of the compromise between Walter and his father.

Warren and Walter weren't close. They had been, once, back when they were children. Back then, folks sometimes even mixed up their names. Now, Warren doubted that they would be recognized as members of the same family, much less brothers.

Warren remembered the first Sunday after Walter had come home from seminary. Their father had proudly surrendered the pulpit. But Walter's sermon... Well, most folks hearing it were merely perplexed, which kept the entire Dunwittee family from being thrown out of church as heretics and reprobates.

Those few who really understood what Walter was preaching had held an emergency meeting after church, to make it clear that Walter was never to preach again in that church. Walter took it poorly, and returned to California. Their father had written often, but sometimes the letters came back, and sometimes they merely vanished.

Warren and Walter had last spoken at the old man's funeral. It hadn't been a friendly conversation. Warren was content to let it go, and to forget that he had ever had a brother.

It was all the more surprising when he found himself thinking of Walter, now. His attitude towards Walter was, as their father had sometimes been inclined to say, "He buttered his bread, and now he can lie in it."

His phone began to ring, so he fished it out of the pocket of his flannel shirt. Probably a telemarketer.

"Hello?" he said, ready to hang up quickly if a recording started.

"Warren?"

His brother's voice startled him, first because it had been so long since they spoke, and secondly because he had just been thinking of him.

"Warren? Is this Warren Dunwittee?"

"Yes, Walter, it's me," he replied, gruffly.

"It's Walt… well, you knew that. I'm just calling to say hello. It's been a while."

"Whose fault is that?"

"Nobody's. Or mine. Call it mine."

"What do you want?"

"I'm hoping we can talk. Like we used to."

"Got kicked out of that church in California?"

"No, no, not at all. But I've… I'm thinking about things, Warren. I was just thinking about Dad."

"You don't have any right to call him that, and you don't have any right or reason to call me at all." With that, Warren hung up the phone.

On Wednesday Night, Mike arrived early for the deacons' meeting. He would give Martin and the pastor fifteen minutes after the hour; if they hadn't arrived by then, he'd say a brief prayer and leave. Since Martin hadn't been in church on Sunday, and Dunwittee usually didn't bother, Mike expected to be alone. Still, he had to go through the motions, just in case.

There was actually a visitors' card to follow up this time. Even if the others didn't do anything, Mike would at least send a postcard. It seemed only courteous, and the least he could do.

Martin came in, a few minutes before the hour.

"Mike, I'm glad to see you," he said, shaking Mike's hand. "I just got in from Big Bear, down in SoCal."

"Have a good trip?"

"Pleasant enough, but more importantly, I got to speak to Susan. We had coffee and talked through some of the things standing between us."

"Buried the hatchet, so to speak?"

"Well, we never really – or at least, I never had any animosity towards her. But before you ask, we're not getting back together. First thing she said to me was, 'I'm in a relationship, so we're not getting back together.' And I'm okay with that."

"Good that you got the ground rules settled at the outset. Then what?"

"I told her that I'm worried about her. About her soul. You know what I mean?"

"I do. And rightly so." This was a side of Martin that Mike hadn't seen for many years, and it took him be surprise. Martin's faith had been so shallow of late, that to hear of him being concerned for a soul was startling.

"I said that I'm not judging, but I felt like she'd gotten far from God. I showed her those photos from snow camp, way back in the nineties."

"What photos?" asked Mike.

Martin produced an envelope of 4x6 photos, and slid it across the desk. Mike slowly thumbed through them, setting some of them aside as he did.

"What year was this?"

"1994, I think," said Martin, pointing to the photo of himself and Susan, sharing an ice cream. "That was the first year we started to like each other."

"I think I went as a counselor that year."

"You did. I remember you being the first person to shake my hand and welcome me into the family of God."

Martin pointed to the photo of himself kneeling, in the old pine chapel. Mike's shoulder could be seen, in the very edge of the photo, where he stood in one of the front rows.

"I remember this," said Mike.

"So did Susan."

"You talked about camp?"

"And about me making a decision without talking to her about it. And about her resenting me being so Jesus-this, Jesus-that."

"She still wound up marrying you."

"Yes, because she thought I'd get over it."

"It sometimes seems like maybe you did, but just a little too late for her."

Martin hung his head. "I've grown cold," he said.

"It's never too late."

"Pastor's sermon the other week, man, it really hit me. Just POW! And I had to go see Susan, you know, and talk it out. So I left right after church."

"That's what, an eight, nine hour drive?"

"Yup. And I got there about ten, you know, stops for coffee and that sort of thing. But we were able to meet and to talk. I don't think she's ready to make a decision for Jesus, but she's at least willing to talk now."

"That's a step in the right direction. We can't save people; you realize that, right?"

"I know, only Jesus can save. All we can do is to point them the right way."

"Do you want me to pray with you?"

Pastor Dunwittee came in just as they were raising their heads and saying "Amen."

"Good, you're both here," he said, taking a seat. "I want to raise an important question, and I want you to answer from the heart. Don't worry about hurting my feelings. I just need your honest answers."

"That haircut stinks," said Martin, with a wink.

"That's not it," said Dunwittee, without missing a beat. "Either I'm losing my mind, or I'm completely off track as a preacher."

"Are those mutually exclusive options?" asked Mike.

"The last few weeks, there's been something badly wrong when I preach."

"I thought your sermons have been improving," said Mike. "In fact, I'm starting to like them."

"That's the problem," said Dunwittee. "What I'm saying is the opposite of what I mean to say. I've become Balaam's donkey."

Mike bit his tongue hard to avoid saying any of the various humorous thoughts that sprang to his mind.

"Your sermon two weeks ago sent me on a mission," said Martin, "To speak the gospel to my ex-wife."

"I didn't mean for that to happen," said Dunwittee.

"Don't apologize," said Martin.

"I'm not." Dunwittee drew a breath. "That Sunday, I meant to speak about how we need to broaden our minds and just accept people as they are, without judging them.

"Instead, I wound up preaching that we have to be very narrow, and we need to bring people to repentance, not acceptance. It was the opposite of what I wanted to say, but I couldn't stop saying it."

"So, what exactly are you saying?" asked Mike.

"I'm saying that after Christmas, when the service is over, I'm going to call the congregation into a business meeting, and submit my resignation."

There was a moment of silence.

"Has another church called you?" asked Martin.

"No, but… Well, I'm getting the strong impression that I could do more for the gospel of Christ if I were to go plant corn."

"I'm cornfused," said Mike. "You're going to take up farming? Growing vegetables?"

"If that's what God wants. Because I'm pretty sure that me, preaching, is not what he wants. I don't think it's what he ever wanted. It's what my father wanted, and what he got for his trouble… Well, I'm going to be frank: I should not be in this pulpit."

"I'm not so sure," said Mike. "When you preach like you did on Sunday, there's power in it. There's a word from God that comes through."

"But it wasn't me. I wasn't in control. God said those words, or at least someone other than me. I was just the vocal chords through which those words came."

"That's how it should be. It should always be God's message through you, and not your thoughts on the matter. You should be completely transparent."

"But here's the thing, I'm not sure I believe what I'm saying. I'm not sure that there's a God whose words I'm meant to speak."

"Wow," said Martin. "In that case, you made a really bad choice of professions."

Mike scratched his chin. "Not trying to be simplistic here, but have you prayed about this?"

Dunwittee started to say, "To whom?" but before the words could escape his mouth, he simply said, "No."

"Lord God," prayed Mike, "Open the pastor's heart and his mind to you. Speak to him as you speak through him, and lead him to your one true path, so that He may enter in at the narrow gate."

"Yes, Lord," prayed Martin.

"Um, God, speak to me and tell me what to do," said Dunwittee.

"Amen," said Mike and Martin, in unison.

"Now what?" asked Dunwittee.

"Now keep doing what you're doing, and we will wait for God to move," said Martin.

As the others left, Mike stayed behind. He wasn't sure when or why things had started to change, but he felt a great confidence in the future, as if some mighty change were on the horizon: A storm, perhaps, but the kind that brings much needed rain.

On an impulse, he pulled down the prayer journal, atop the bookshelf, and flicked it open to a random page.

Tonight, as I thought about the life and brief ministry of our Lord and Savior, I felt inspired to write this:

Borrowed Manger, Borrowed Tomb;
This world refused to own
A Savior come, mankind to save
Through faith in Him alone

Borrowed Grace, and Borrowed Faith;
Oh, this is all I own:
My Savior came, mankind to save
Through faith, in Him, alone.

Mike read it twice. Then he closed the journal and put it back on top of the bookshelf.

Chapter Nine

ROME WAS NOT BUILT in a single day, nor does a single shot win a war. Pastor Dunwittee, for all of the conviction under which he had fallen, was not entirely convinced that he had fallen into the hands of God.

Of the hypotheses that went through his mind, one was that Mike was a hypnotist, and had conditioned him to say the opposite of what he felt. Mike was certainly enjoying the outcome, and what had been happening to him was entirely in line with Mike's vision of the church.

Also, the call to Warren had gone very badly. He couldn't imagine Warren reacted any better than that to a phone call, and he didn't know why he had even reached out to him. But if he were to go back to the traditional way of doing things, one part of that was to make things right – something in one of the epistles, about living rightly with all, so far as it depends upon you. But he really couldn't control how Warren would react to that.

He still didn't know why he kept saying words he didn't mean to say during the sermons. He told himself that his reaction during the sermon – the thought that he had become Balaam's donkey – was merely something physical happening inside him. Perhaps it was indigestion, or a reaction to the chamomile tea he'd had that morning. It might even be a twinge of guilt about his father.

Conversations with Warren often made him feel badly, so why would this one be any different? Warren had thought their father was some sort of a giant, or a hero, but in reality he was just an average ranch hand. Still, Walter could have been nicer to him, maybe.

But regardless what had caused him to do it, that reaction in the pulpit was just something in his mind, like a record skipping a groove. It wasn't real – he had been taught that nothing which happens in a person's mind is ever real, so of course the feeling of being a donkey could not possibly have been real.

Within a few hours after the deacons' meeting, he had rationalized the entire thing. He would continue on with his sermon series – the shepherds were up next. And he would very carefully avoid eye contact with Mike, to keep from being mesmerized into giving the opposite of his prepared sermon. Careful preparation and careful delivery. Those would be the keys.

Thursday morning found Martin at Dorman's café. Mr. Fenwick was a few minutes late, but Martin waved him over as he came in. He was a tall man with a very casual and yet professional air about him. His skin was like coffee with a bit of milk added to it.

"Mr. Fenwick," said Martin, rising slightly from his seat. "I'm Martin."

"Please, call me Garth."

"Thanks for calling back. I'm glad you were able to meet with me today."

"Well, I'm kind of glad you called. We tried two other churches in the area, but neither contacted us at all. It was as if we didn't exist."

"I'm sorry to hear that, but I'm glad you visited with us. Do you live locally?"

"We just moved from Smyrna. My wife, Faith, is originally from Philadelphia."

"What brings you to Sardis?"

"My job. I'm going to be a manager at the new tire plant, south of town."

"That looks like a nice facility. When do they expect to start production?"

"Late Winter, early Spring, if things go well. We still need to hire a lot of the staff we'll need. And we'll have to transfer some key people from other plants."

"That's great. If I hear of people looking for work, I'll point them to you." About then, the waitress came around with cups of coffee, and took orders for their omelets. Garth took his with sourdough toast, and Martin opted for the English Muffin.

"Faith calls those crumpets," remarked Garth. "She's a big fan of English tea cozy mysteries, and I think it's affected her vocabulary."

"To each her own," said Martin. "So were you guys involved in a church in Smyrna?"

"First Baptist Smyrna. It's a small church, like yours. Not very much in the budget, but we were able to do a lot with it. Folks sacrificed their time and effort to make things happen. Wonderful fellowship."

"I've heard good things."

"Faith was saved as a teenager, at a Bible camp near Philadelphia. We met in college. I was raised in a Christian home, and baptized when I was ten. After college, we moved back to Smyrna, I got a job at the tire plant, and here we are."

"Do you have children?"

"Just the twins, Clarissa and Marissa," Garth said, as the waitress slid hot plates of food in front of them. "They were staying with Faith's parents for Thanksgiving, but you'll meet them next Sunday."

"I look forward to seeing all of you there," said Martin, tasting his eggs and adding a bit of salt. And then a bit more. And finally a healthy coating of black pepper.

Garth sipped his coffee. "Are there many children in the church?"

"Mainly just one family. The Cannons. I believe that they only have three, but the way the kids dart around, it sometimes looks like more. Did you meet them Sunday?"

"We had to run, a thing with my family over in Smyrna. We didn't have a chance to meet many folks."

"I'll introduce you on Sunday," said Martin.

At about that same time, Mike was at work, in his office cubicle, working on insurance rate adjustments. He was, as the work implies, an insurance rate adjuster by profession. It was not glamourous work, but it paid his bills and kept him fed.

As too often happened, his concentration was broken by a passerby.

"Hey, Mike," said George, the Actuarial, as he leaned against the doorway of Mike's cubicle. "Did you hear about that bus crash in Castroville?"

"No," said Mike. He would have followed that with a curt statement about being too busy to hear about it now, except that George had already begun spilling the lurid details. So, instead, he politely waited for George to take a breath before interrupting.

"That's interesting," said Martin. "But I've got…"

"You're a Christian, aren't you?"

"Yes, I'm a deacon at my church. But that's…"

"So why does God let things like that happen?"

"Well, without deacons, we'd have no one to take care of the widows and orphans."

"No, I mean bus crashes."

"Bad things happen because we live in a fallen world. And they sometimes happen to good people who don't deserve them. That's the multiplying effect of sin. Each sin leads to more sin, and the net effect is bad things. Bus crashes, accidents, violence."

"So, if that's true, how come we haven't just fallen into utter chaos already?"

"Because grace also multiplies, and cancels sin. Suppose you hit me. Or rob me. Or interrupt me while I'm working. If I take revenge, and do the same back to you, sin multiplies, because I'm sinning to avenge your sin. And so on.

"But if I forgive you, then grace multiplies instead. I forgive you, you forgive others, and that pattern spreads instead. Grace conquers sin, even in a fallen world."

George took a step back. "That's not a bad answer. Sin and grace, fighting for dominance. I don't believe in sin, but it's a nice concept. Very neat."

"Glad you like it. If you don't mind, I've got some charts to finish…"

"Right." George wandered away. Mike resolved to pray for him, and went back to his adjustments.

Sunday came suddenly, and found Pastor Dunwittee very badly prepared. He still intended to speak about shepherds, and the importance of shepherds to the Christ-myth, but he hadn't fleshed out the full text.

He supposed he would *ad lib* the rest, and make it up as he went along. He doubted anyone would notice. He made his usual pre-service rounds, peeking into the children's wing, where Mrs. Henson had the children sword-fighting. He closed the door and...

Sword-fighting?

He opened the door quickly, to find the children paired off, hacking at each other with swords. None of the steel seemed to find flesh; the children were quite content to bang the blades together.

"Mrs. Henson," he called out, "Is that safe?"

"Oh, Pastor," she said with a grin, "When I was a girl, we did sword drills every Sunday. And no one was ever hurt by it."

She clapped her hands. "Children, let's show the pastor what we've learned."

The children formed a single line, facing Dunwittee. There were two new children that he didn't recognize, somewhere in age between Alyssa and Efrem.

Five children, all facing him with drawn swords. It was a bit frightening, truth be told. Where had they gotten the swords?

"These were in the closet, behind the baptistry," said Efrem. "I told you there were lots of them!"

"Emily," said Mrs. Henson, "You drill them."

"Attention," said Emily, from her place in the line. The children all stood straight, swords pointed at the floor. "Salute," she said, and as one, they whipped the swords up to their noses, pointed skyward.

Efrem had his sword turned so that the edge was towards his face. Mrs. Henson gently reached over his head and turned his hand ninety degrees.

"Two!" said Emily, and the children whipped their blades down and to the right, in a smooth curve.

Dunwittee found himself uncharacteristically without words. It was at once impressive and terrifying. Children with sharp, two-edged swords. Oh, the damage they could do, if they were so inclined!

"Thank you, Mrs. Henson," he said, quietly retreating and closing the door behind him. He would need to have a word with the deacons about this. Things were getting out of hand.

The song service – well, the choice of music was still a bit too much on-point for his taste: Traditional old hymns of joy to the world, and angels singing, little towns with secret treasures in them, and stars marking a literal Savior, born as a baby.

Still, it was tradition, and couched in that older English form that made it hard to understand today. He doubted that any of the children would know what "Hail th'incarnate Deity" would mean.

"Mom," stage-whispered Efrem, at just that moment, "What does th'incarnate mean?"

"It means God in human flesh," Lupe whispered back. "God became a little baby."

A rousing chorus covered any counter-comment that Efrem may have made. Dunwittee gritted his teeth. It was as if everything in the world were against him; as if the universe itself were shaped wrongly for him to express his ideas to these people.

"Today, I see that we have lit the shepherds' candle," said Dunwittee. That phrase was something he had actually meant to say. He paused for a moment, to see if unintentional words would start pouring out of his mouth.

When none were forthcoming, he smiled to himself and tried his next point. "Shepherds, the humblest of humans, were the first to hear of the great blessings of God," he said.

That was not what he had meant to say. He carefully kept his eyes on the papers in front of him, to keep Mike from mesmerizing him. But it appeared to be too late.

"A humble Savior, God in the flesh, found of all places, in a borrowed manger. This sign, the great and holy God condescending to become a helpless baby, is a foreshadow, if you will, of that same holy God, creator of all things, by whom and for whom the galaxies spin their courses, condescending to die on a cross and to lay in a borrowed tomb.

"I heard a poem the other day; I don't know where it's from:

"Borrowed manger, borrowed tomb,
This world refused to own
A Savior come mankind to save
Through faith in Him alone.

"Borrowed Grace and borrowed Faith,
Oh, this is all I own:
My Savior came, mankind to save
Through faith in him alone."

Mike's eyes widened. He knew where it was from: It was in the prayer journal. He had read from it just the other night. Could it be Pastor Dunwittee's prayer journal? Mike dismissed that thought: Whoever wrote that journal had a completely different mind; one set on God and not on self-actualization.

"Friends," said Dunwittee, "Let us not take lightly the condescension of God: That just as we are told in Philippians 2, He first laid aside His glory and was made into a man, and then a servant, and finally the subject of a crucifixion, faithful unto death, even death on the cross. All of this, for us, for our salvation."

It is a very profound thought, said Mike to himself. *The Word becoming flesh and dwelling among us.*

"In John 1:14, we find that the Word became flesh, and pitched his tent alongside ours," said Dunwittee, "God in our very midst, just as in the days when Israel wandered in the wilderness. God beside us; God our friend; God our neighbor.

"So why should it surprise us that he was heralded, not by courtiers in fancy clothes, in a palace, but by simple shepherds, fresh from the fields, and surrounded by their charges? People like us, in other words."

Dunwittee looked around the room, seeing upturned faces, eyes deep in thought. He wished that he could provoke that same sort of contemplation when he told them to love themselves, and that God desired, above all else, their happiness.

Perhaps they just weren't ready for the sorts of messages that were within him. They would rather stick to traditions and old ways.

"If you find yourself needing a shepherd to direct your ways," said Dunwittee, "If you are searching for a star to guide you; If you earnestly desire that the Son of God come into your life and pitch his tent in your heart, then come forward and let us pray with you."

He motioned for Mike and for Martin to stand with him in the front.

After the service, Faith Fenwick approached Mike. She was the wife of Garth Fenwick. She was a very pretty woman, with ebony skin and bright teeth. Her hair was long and straight, and she had a small nose that drew attention to her deep brown eyes.

"You have an interesting way of doing the music," she said. "I suppose that it makes it simple that way."

"Well," said Mike, "In the land of the tone-deaf, I am the one-eared man. I do the best I can with what meager talents I have."

"I've never heard it put like that," she said. "If I can help, I'd be glad to lead sometimes. I used to lead the music at Smyrna Baptist."

"That would be wonderful," said Mike.

"Now, does anyone in the congregation play any musical instruments?"

"Mrs. Henson used to play the piano," said Mike. "But that was a long time ago."

"I don't suppose that you'd introduce me?"

"I'd love to," said Mike.

---

1. *Veiled in flesh, the Godhead see; / Hail th'Incarnate deity* are lines from Charles Wesley's 1739 hymn, *Hark the Herald Angels Sing.*

Chapter Ten

"IT'S SO LUCKY THAT you called," purred Dr. Lykos. "Of course I remember you, Walter."

Dr. Vorace Lykos was perhaps a generation or so older than pastor Dunwittee, and had begun to go gray at the temples. He felt that this gave him an air of authority.

He seemed oddly lupine, at times. He was a fairly short man, perhaps five-nine or five-ten, and he made up for his small stature by being vicious and fierce. Even today, in a calm conversation, it seemed to Dunwittee that Lykos was growling at him.

"Thank you, Dr. Lykos. It's just that, well, things have been a bit odd lately... I feel that I'm somehow going far afield in my sermons."

"You've been reminding them to love themselves, right? Self-care, self-acceptance, self-praise? Affirmations every morning?"

"That's just it. I always intend to say that sort of thing, but once I'm in the pulpit, I –"

"Feel pressured? To conform? To fit in, and go along with the dogma?"

That wasn't exactly what Dunwittee meant, but he did feel pressure. It wasn't pressure from the church, like Lykos meant, but it was definitely pressure. And it wouldn't do to contradict Dr. Lykos. He could be very mean when one didn't agree with him.

"Yes, in a way."

"Sounds like they need a stern rebuke," said Lykos. "As it happens, I'll be in your area next Sunday. I'd love an invitation to preach."

"But, of course, Dr. Lykos," said Dunwittee. "It would be an honor."

"I'll even waive my honorarium," he said, "Since I doubt those old fuddy-duddies would want to be sternly rebuked and then have to pay for it."

"That would be most kind," said Dunwittee. He suddenly had the feeling of being very small, like a child, asking an adult for a privilege. It wasn't a feeling he liked, and it made him glad that Lykos didn't live closely enough to make this offer all the time.

"I'll see you, then, at nine AM sharp." Lykos hung up the phone. Dunwittee felt, at once, both a feeling of dread and a feeling of relief. Next Sunday he would be free from the burden of preparing a sermon that he wouldn't be able to give. And yet, being back under the thumb of Dr. Lykos was a frightening thought.

Dunwittee smiled to himself. "Let's see if Mike can mesmerize Lykos," he said, aloud. "That'll teach him to enchant me!"

Faith Fenwick found the key on the ground, just next to the door. She could hardly have missed it. It gleamed so brightly that it seemed to have been polished.

Curiosity got the better of her, and she used it to open the door. On the single shelf, stacked in neat rows, were dozens of songbooks. She picked one up.

Modern Worship Songs for Today's Churches, she read. Well, that was certainly convenient. She flicked it open to the copyright page, and found that it had been published in 2022. *And relegated to a closet already,* she thought, clucking her tongue. *Now all we need is a license agreement…*

She turned a leaf, and a slip of paper fluttered out from between two pages. She bent to pick it up, and found that she was holding a receipt in the name of the church. The license agreement, it seemed, was good through 2024, and renewable thereafter.

She smiled. *YHWH-Jireh,* she thought. *The LORD will provide.*

Lupe Cannon was wrangling the children back into the car, after their stop at a fast-food restaurant. Luis sat behind the wheel.

"Hey, Babe," he said, when she at last slid into her seat. "I spoke to Mrs. Henson."

"Alyssa, put on your seatbelt." She turned and gave Luis her attention. "And what did she say?"

"She would love to have the children come over next Friday. She said that she would show them how to make sugar cookies."

"Oh, can we, Mom?" asked Emily. "It was tons of fun last Friday! She showed us how to play cribbage."

"Cribbage and cookies," said Lupe. "Next thing you know, our children will have lots of new hobbies."

"I don't know how we'll fill the time until they return," said Luis. "We might have to sit in the dark and eat cold spaghetti."

"Oh, right," said Efrem, with a grin. "Last time you guys went to a restaurant."

"We didn't get to go," said Alyssa, with a nagging pout in her voice.

"It wasn't the fun kind," said Efrem. "It was the kind where you have to be quiet and eat with the right fork."

Alyssa was scandalized by the idea of a "right" fork. That also meant that there might be a wrong fork, and how would one know a wrong fork from a right one? *Why would someone even keep a fork that was wrong?* That sobering thought – that a fork might be wrong – kept her in quiet contemplation for the rest of the ride home. Her mind was abuzz. *What would a wrong fork even look like? And were there also wrong spoons and knives?*

Dunwittee was also thinking of wrong forks, but in a different way. It seemed to him that perhaps, possibly, the path of his life had taken a wrong fork. If Warren could be happy with a simple life, fixing tractors in small-town Texas, why couldn't Walter?

He knew the answer: He had dreamed of more. He had dreamed of making a mark on the world, by radically changing how people saw themselves and how they saw the world around them. But the world wasn't like that.

The reality was that he was spinning his wheels, biding his time, searching for a place and a time that might not ever happen. *Is this,* he asked himself, *the day for which I was born, and the hour against which I was conceived?*

A day away; that was what he needed. And there was a holiday coming up; Why, of all the days of the year, couldn't he just take Christmas off? He'd explain to the deacons that it was a necessary day of rest. He could contemplate where he was in life, and where his life should be going.

Maybe he'd go camping. Christmas was often nice in California, and he'd heard of a state park he wanted to try, at Mount Diablo. But he probably wouldn't mention it to Mike or Martin just yet.

Mrs. Henson was humming to herself as she made a quick lunch and a cup of tea. It had been a lovely service. She wondered if the Bible drills were really enough for the children. Perhaps they should all begin some sort of Bible study plan. Something structured. Not necessarily the old Sunday School quarterlies, but something relatable for the kids. Maybe a theme, like the Vacation Bible School kind of thing. That might be fun.

She resolved that she would look up some good Bible materials right after lunch. In truth, she intended to. Without a doubt, she had every intention of that very thing. And then, the phone rang.

Mike returned to his home after a hearty lunch with the Fenwicks. No sooner had he kicked off his shoes and settled into his recliner than there was a knock at the door. He peeked out through the glass and saw Mrs. Henson standing on the porch, still wearing her best hat, beaded purse in hand.

"Mrs. Henson," he started to say, but she cut him off sharply, holding up one finger.

"No time to explain," she declared. "Put on your shoes and let's go."

"Go where?"

"Lillian Boswell's house," said Mrs. Henson. "Her mother just passed, and she's distraught."

As they piled into Mike's pickup, to set out on their mission of mercy, Mike had a thought. "Mrs. Henson," he asked, "How did you get here? You don't usually drive this far."

"Oh, I just walked," she said. "It's such a very nice afternoon and all."

"It must be five miles to your house."

"Mike," she said, shaking her head, "Haven't you read Isaiah 40:31? We shall run and not grow weary; we shall walk and not grow faint."

"I'll remember that the next time my bones creak as I get out of a chair."

"Mike, the Lord will give you strength in your old age, and he will bless your soul with the latter rains. Just you wait and see."

She closed her lips, but smiled behind them, as someone who is trying not to laugh at a private joke. It made Mike wonder what Mrs. Henson was up to. Also, if she could so easily walk five miles to Mike's house, and not be out of breath, what stopped her from walking two more miles to Lillian's house?

At the Boswell home, they found a cluster of cars; some belonging to mourners and some to those intending comfort. Mike parked carefully, with the front of his car pointed towards the road.

He didn't begrudge Mrs. Henson the ride, and visits to the grieving were certainly within a Deacon's duties, but he did wonder why he was there. Mrs. Henson knew the Boswells far better than he did, and her presence would be a thousand times the comfort he might offer. Also, the Boswells were members of the local Methodist church, so his presence might be seen as intrusive.

After they were admitted, and he found himself in the dining room, standing among a group of men he didn't know at all, the reason became apparent. There, speaking softly to a man whom Mike took to be a minister of some sort, was George the actuarial.

George spotted Mike and nodded. He patted the minister on the shoulder and worked his way through the crowd to Mike's side.

"How do you know the Boswells?" asked Mike, in a voice barely above a whisper.

"Marriage," he said. "Lucy is Lillian's half-sister."

Mike resisted the urge to ask if two half-sisters made one whole sister. Under the circumstances, it would just be wrong, and he was ashamed to have thought it.

"Ah," he said, instead.

"Look, I know I give you grief in the office. You know, about God and all. But it really means a lot that you're here. You know. That it's more than just talk."

"Mrs. Henson brought me," he said. "But I didn't know why until now."

The two men talked for a while; at first of lighter, mostly trivial things, and then slowly of the tragedy at hand, and finally, after some considerable time had passed, they began to speak of deeper things.

Mourners and comforters came and went; food was brought in and sent out; hands were shaken and tears were wept, and still they talked.

After a while a woman came over to them, whose careful outfit and demeanor was only broken by the redness of her eyes. George slipped his arm around her shoulders.

"Lucy, this is Mike, from work. I've mentioned him."

"How do you do?" she asked, offering him her fingertips and a thin smile.

"I'm well," he said. "But how are you?"

Lucy pursed her lips, dabbed at her eyes with a well-crumpled tissue, and nodded softly.

"Mike's a deacon at Sardis Baptist," said George. "He brought Mrs. Henson."

"Oh," said Lucy. "She used to teach us in vacation Bible school when we were little. So very long ago." She looked up at her husband. "So sweet of her to come."

She held her husband's eye for a moment, expressing to him, without words, her weariness and the need to be away from the noise.

"We should go," said George. "Thank you again for being here, Mike."

"You're welcome," said Mike. "And call me if … well, you know."

Mrs. Henson appeared next to his elbow almost the moment George and Lucy were out the door. "It's far too late for an old lady like me to be out and about," she said. "People will talk. Now take me home right away."

The midweek service came too quickly for everyone, and especially Pastor Dunwittee. In fact, the rapid pace of services made it seem as if he had only barely recovered from one service before another was upon him.

This might account for the lateness of his arrival. It would have made no difference, however, had he been on time, or even a few minutes early. Long before he arrived, the service had spontaneously started.

It began around five, when Mike had looked at his watch and had seen the wrong time. It was barely even five, but he hurried down to the church nonetheless, believing it was nearly six.

Hardly had he opened the doors when folks began to arrive. Mrs. Henson came first, followed quickly by the Fenwicks, and then the Cannons. Others, in ones and twos and families, filtered in behind those, until by five-thirty, some twenty-five individuals were there.

This was well above the norm: If Mike could count a dozen on Wednesday Night, one for each disciple, he considered it a good meeting. Were there thirteen, then the last supper, or the baker's-dozen tribes of Israel came to mind. But tonight, it didn't seem even slightly odd that two dozen and more had assembled.

It was over an hour before the posted start time, but Mrs. Henson didn't wait. She sternly called everyone into a season of silent prayer. From time to time, an individual would speak out, calling out to God for a specific request, before again falling silent.

Martin recalled similar prayer sessions, from his teen years. Back then, the leaders had called it "popcorn prayer," as if those calling out to God were like kernels of corn, randomly bursting out from within.

In the stillness there was a feeling of peace, and of community; a church come together in common cause. And then a voice was heard that made Martin's eyes open in shock.

"O Lord, I have been far from Thee," said Susan. "I have wandered far afield, like a sheep that goes astray. Cleanse me with hyssop, and I shall be pure; wash me in Thy blood, that I may be clean."

"Amen," whispered Martin, with tears in his eyes. "Lord God, hear this prayer."

One of the ladies of the church went to her and put an arm around her, and began to pray with her.

One by one, people spoke their petitions to God. Each petition was met with murmurs of "Yes, Lord," and "Amen," as others joined their hearts to those in need.

Between prayers aloud, the silence was not awkward. Even the children felt the solemnity of the moment, and were still before God, waiting for Him to move.

It was into this environment that Dunwittee arrived. It seemed to him, at first glance, that he saw actual smoke rising from the congregants; visible vapor, like some form of incense, rising to the Holy One.

No, it was not smoke; it was something smoke-like and far more numinous, far more powerful. His legs weakened. He was seeing prayers again, as he had seen with the lantern. He was seeing petitions rising to God.

The scent of the prayers, like sweet incense, like an intoxicating mist, and made his nostrils tingle. He became aware of an otherworldly Presence, to Whom the prayers flowed; a Holiness that was both set apart, terribly so, and yet approachable, all at once. It drew him in and pushed him down, as if to fall on his knees.

It was only the sheer strength of his will that kept him from running away. He drew himself upright, despite the powerful urge to fall prostrate. He closed his eyes and opened them; the smoke was gone.

It had surely been an illusion, a hallucination, a figment of his imagination. The feeling of a holy presence was quenched, and while he was relieved by this, he found his heart pounding in his chest.

He stood quietly, and then worked his way around the kneeling group, until he could reach the rostrum. When there had been a gap of a few minutes without a spoken prayer, he spoke.

"As you finish your prayers, go ahead and return to your seats," he said. "We have a lot of ground to cover tonight. We're running late, and we need to address the importance of the Christ-myth."

No one seemed to hear him. Their heads remained bowed, their eyes closed, in concentration upon the One who hears prayers. No one looked up; no one except Alyssa, whose eyes met his with laser-like focus.

"That's not how you say it," she snapped at him. "It's not Chritht-myth. It's Christmas!"

Her head bowed again, leaving Dunwittee facing a room full of people who were unaware of his presence.

The little girl's rebuke shattered his resolve; he worked his way around them and nearly ran for the door. If they really wanted to hold a prayer meeting, he would let them do it.

Just then a thought popped into his mind.

As if you could stop them.

Chapter Eleven

"OF GRACE AND THE KING, I sing," intoned Mrs. Henson, reciting her original composition with all the solemnity and projection of a classical Greek chorus. "Who came, compelled by Love, self-exiled out of heaven; To Earth and the Bethlehem plain, to endure the buffeting of sin's penalties, and to deliver to Death dark defeat and doom."

She turned and nodded to Efrem, who held open a battered old Bible that had seen too many Sunday schools and VBS classes.

"The people that walked in darkness have seen a great light," he read. "They that dwell in the land of the shadow of death, upon them hath the light shined."

He put down the Bible and quickly took his place on the stage. Alyssa stood in the center, flanked by the Fenwick twins, while Efrem and Emily stood on the riser immediately behind them, to be seen over them.

During the reading of Isaiah 9:2, Mrs. Henson had made her way to the piano, where she struck a note and gave the children a significant look. The note was meant to tell the children in what key they should sing, but to the children it was merely something one did before playing a song on the piano. They stood silently, waiting for Mrs. Henson to give them the nod.

Mrs. Henson began to play, and after a moment, nodded to the children. In a slightly broken chorus that more or less followed the tune, and more or less kept the right time, the children began to sing *O Come All Ye Faithful.* She played at about three-quarters of the normal tempo, to give the children a fair chance to keep up.

When at long last, they came to the final chorus, the congregation applauded generously. Mrs. Henson cleared her throat, and began waving her hand in the same tempo that she had just played. With an exaggerated nod, she began to sing, and the children, tentatively and haltingly, followed her through one last verse, *a cappella.*

"Adeste fideles, laeti triumphanti,
Venite, venite in Bethlehem.
Natum vedite, Regum angelorum,
Venite adoremas, venite adoremas;
Venite adoremas, Dominium."

The church, slightly awestruck, was silent for a moment, and then applauded again, more vigorously than before. Mrs. Henson had somehow not only taught the children the carol, but in Latin as well.

"They should do that every week," said one of the older ladies, loudly, in what she meant for a stage whisper to her neighbor. It carried to the far corners of the room.

"I can't get them to say *con permiso* when they walk in front of someone, and she's got them singing in Latin? How does she do it?" murmured Lupe to Luis.

Mrs. Henson clapped her hands one time. Her little charges stood straight and cleared their throats. She began to play *Angels We Have Heard On High*, and the children, now over their initial stage fright, kept better time and approached something akin to harmony. Mrs. Henson joined in on the choruses, at first joining her soprano to the children's voices in unison.

On the final chorus, she soared above them in a high alto that lent an unearthly feel to the piece, causing several of the church members to shiver with goosebumps.

This time, when the piano stopped, everyone stood and applauded. Even Dunwittee stood, though he felt trapped into it. His applause was soft and half-hearted.

Mrs. Henson pointed to the front of the platform. The children, in a halting movement that was clearly under-rehearsed, lined up at the edge. Efrem suddenly realized that he was in the wrong spot, pulled back, and ducked between Alyssa and Emily, pushing into place.

When they were finally aligned properly, with Efrem between his sisters, so that he wouldn't be next to girls he didn't know, they all clasped hands and took a bow.

The church, once again, was thoroughly delighted, and again applauded. The children, relieved to be finished, made their way down and joined their parents.

That, thought Dunwittee, *Was surely the oddest Christmas program that I've ever seen. But I'd better not comment: They might try to fix it.*

"I see that we have lit the Angels' candle today," said Dunwittee, "And, indeed, weren't our children just little angels today?"

No, they were most certainly not, thought Mike. *Angels are huge and frighteningly fierce. People tremble on seeing them. The children were not the least bit scary; quite the opposite. But it was a wonderful music program.*

"By the purest of good luck," continued Dunwittee, "I was fortunate enough to be in touch with my old professor from Seminary, Dr. Vorace Lykos. He has very graciously offered to speak today, and so it is with very great pleasure that I yield the podium to him."

Dunwittee passed Dr. Lykos in the aisle. Dunwittee's morning coffee picked that moment to expire, so he quietly made his way down the side aisle and out the back, into the foyer.

Dr. Lykos smiled and turned his head, revealing a broad and gleaming array of white teeth. It struck Mike that perhaps they looked a bit too pointed, as if he might possibly have more than the normal number of canines.

"Pastor Dunwittee is very kind," he said. "I am, as he mentioned, a professor at the Santa Cruz Seminary of Spiritual Matters, or, as we like to call it, Spirit Matters.

"Now, today, we're focused on this somewhat dubious story of angels hovering over Bethlehem, singing God to sleep. I'm not going to read it to you. I didn't bring my Bible today."

Had Dunwittee been listening, and not taking care of personal business, he would not have been surprised to hear that Lykos hadn't brought a Bible. Lykos' disdain for scripture was well known among his students.

In fact, it was slightly disingenuous of Lykos to phrase it that way, since it implied that, had he not been so rushed, he might have brought a Bible. That was simply not true. Lykos would never have opened a Bible of his own free will.

Lykos looked around the room at the calm faces before him. They clearly had no inkling of what he was up to, and it would be so much fun to shatter their beliefs. He very nearly laughed to himself.

"Angels," he began, with that toothy smile, ignoring the little boy who was coming up the outside aisle. "Well, what are we supposed to make of angels? These flying people, not exactly visible, but sometimes visible... I mean, they just appear from nowhere – egad, Lad! What are you doing?"

It was at this point that Dunwittee re-entered the auditorium, and was startled to find Efrem standing on the platform with a large, shiny sword. It might have been the one he had confiscated from the boy, several weeks before. Had the boy found it again?

The boy, with boldness and confidence, seemed to be repelling a growling wolf, who was slowly backing away towards the door to the offices. A wolf, an actual wolf, with claws and teeth. In the church.

"Everyone just remain calm," murmured Dunwittee, mostly to himself. The people watched, not even blinking at the spectacle.

The boy brandished the sword, in what appeared to be a clever katana kata, involving steps, chops, lunges, swipes, and stabbing thrusts. The wolf, yelping when the blade drew too near, was now on the very farthest edge of the platform.

Efrem lunged once more at him, and the wolf, with a whimpering whine, quit the stage and dashed out through the door to the offices, as fast as four legs could carry him away from the scene.

Dunwittee blinked; the sword became a Bible, and Efrem was holding it towards the people, bewildered.

"He said he forgot his Bible," said Efrem. "I was just going to give him mine..." For lack of a better thing to do with it, he placed it onto the podium.

In the silence that followed, Dunwittee strode up the center aisle and took the podium, waving Efrem back to his seat. It appeared that he would need to preach after all, and he was wholly unprepared.

"It appears that Doctor Lykos has suddenly taken ill," said Dunwittee. "And unfortunately, I don't have a sermon prepared." He tried to think of something clever to say about angels. And then, suddenly, the words were no longer his.

"Angels, who gathered and sang at the birth of Jesus," said Dunwittee. "How very puzzled they must have been, just a few years later, to see the Creator-God of the whole universe, dying on a cross, rejected by all the world, and left to die like the foulest of criminals."

He paused, and allowed his words to take effect. "A single angel, as we learn from 2 Kings 19:35, has incredible power. In that passage, one angel slew 185,000 armed men. It would only have taken one angel to rescue Jesus, but Jesus told Peter that more than 12 legions of angels were at His disposal.

"Legions, which, in Jesus time, would have meant five thousand foot soldiers, with another several hundred horsemen and auxiliaries. Twelve of them, or more than 60,000 angels, in total, all at Jesus' command.

"If we simply take those numbers, there were enough angels available to Jesus to have slain everyone in Israel, and in most of that region. Possibly even the entire population of the earth at that time.

"But that is not what Jesus did. We find in Philippians 2, that having humbled Himself to be a human; and having humbled Himself to become a servant, a lowly human who washed the feet of the disciples; He humbled himself further to allow Himself to be treated with the most humiliating of contempt, and finally to be executed as a criminal by humans whom He, Himself, had made."

Dunwittee drew a breath. "Indeed, when we see the angels' candle, let us think of angels; let us consider how very odd those angels found the breathtaking humility of this little Baby, almighty God."

He closed the Bible that Efrem had left open.

Unprompted, the congregation, in unison, began to sing the chorus, "O Come let us adore him," as Mrs. Henson, adjusting the tempo to fit, began to sing the chorus of the other hymn.

Mike blinked in surprise at how well *Gloria in excelsis Deo* could be fitted with *Come let us adore him*. It was what the young people called a mash-up, and impromptu though it was, it worked perfectly.

The congregation continued to sing as they gathered their things and filed out of the auditorium.

Mike waited for the aisle to clear, and then walked over to the pastor, who looked vaguely as if he might pass out at any moment.

"That was a lovely service," he said.

"I assure you, I had nothing to do with it," said Dunwittee. Dunwittee was tempted to ask Mike if Mike had seen the wolf and the sword, or if he had merely seen a little boy offer a man a Bible.

He knew that he couldn't ask. If Mike had seen what he had seen – a little boy protecting the flock from a wolf by brandishing a sharp and shiny sword – that would imbue it with a sense of reality for which Dunwittee was simply not prepared.

Ordinarily, one is comforted to find that one is not hallucinating, but Dunwittee was comforting himself with the idea that his mind was simply playing tricks on him. If it were all a dream, then he need not explain it.

The service itself, frightening as it had been, was not nearly so terrifying as the only real explanation that came to mind, namely, that the one true God, whose name he had been carelessly casting about for these many years, was very real and was manifesting Himself in this place.

"It was, whether by your efforts or not, a lovely service," repeated Mike. "But that's not why I came over to speak to you. We're baptizing Emily next week, and we need to make arrangements."

"Arrr," said Dunwittee. "Ah. Yes, of course, Emily's baptism. Right."

He had forgotten the baptism. There was only a week to prepare, and he had not the slightest idea what would be expected. He had managed, over his entire career as a pastor, never to actually baptize anyone.

"Is it possible," asked Dunwittee, "That either you or Martin might do the actual immersion? I'm feeling a bit of a cold coming on, and I'd hate to pass it along."

"A cold?" asked Mike. He peered into Dunwittee's eye, which seemed perfectly clear and bright, and not the least bit red or rheumy.

Dunwittee cleared his throat, as if to support the idea that he wasn't entirely healthy at that moment. "Ah, you know, just, possibly a touch of a cold… Hard to say, at the moment…" Dunwittee's cell phone began to ring, and he looked at it with relief. "I'm sorry, I'm going to have to take this," he continued.

Mike stared after him in disbelief as he ducked through the door, towards the offices.

Dunwittee's relief was short-lived. The call was from Dr. Lykos, and he was livid.

"I don't know what you think you're playing at," Lykos began, "But I am not amused. That boy attacked me; he positively came after me with a sword – an honest to goodness sword."

"I'm sure he didn't know…"

"You can't excuse it," snapped Lykos. "A boy! With a sword! Charging across the platform at me like Roland at Ronceveaux! How dare you?"

"Honestly, he just wanted to give you…"

"Give me a few hacks with that sharp blade? Cut out my heart? Give me something, Dunwittee? Give me a break! You need to get control of those people, before they do something truly insane."

Lykos hung up.

Getting control of this church was not even on Dunwittee's agenda, not in the least. If he couldn't even control his own tongue long enough to preach a simple Sunday sermon, it was very irrational to suggest that he control the congregation. If he had had any doubts about his lack of control over the church, the last few services made it very obvious.

It crossed Dunwittee's mind to go in the opposite direction, and to do something truly over-the-top in order to help the church see where their fanaticism was dragging them. He supposed he might, oh, maybe do something obscure, like a foot-washing service. No, that was a gesture of humility. It went against trying to make them into their own authentic selves.

Or, better still; bring rattlesnakes to handle at the next Wednesday Night service. That would certainly stir them up a bit. And after the way they had ignored him the previous Wednesday, they deserved it.

They had ignored their own pastor, and just kept praying as if he hadn't been there at all. As if prayer were more important than what he had been trying to do.

He wondered where he might find rattlesnakes.

Unfortunately, the sheer impracticality of the idea kept him from trying his hand at snake-handling. Where would he get them and what would he do if they bit him?

While the adults were busy chattering amongst themselves, as adults are wont to do following a service, Alyssa ran to the closet door and inserted the key. The door practically sprang open as she touched it.

There, on the shelf, were two forks. One of them was silvery and ornate, with a very shiny handle and four precise tines, all even and perfectly aligned. It was the sort of fork that was most obviously the right fork.

To the left of it was a very different sort of utensil. The tines were bent, and the outside pair met, point to point, making a sort of a loop. The inside pair went high and low past the loop, before themselves meeting in the middle. With the tines so joined, it would be impossible to push them into anything, such as a piece of meat or a slice of potato.

And with the tines making an odd crisscross, there would be no way to scoop up vegetables. Peas would roll right under the raised center tine, or else roll down the drooping center tine, and either way, you'd never get them to your mouth.

There was no way anyone could be fed by such a twisted utensil as this. It was – yes, of course! That was a wrong fork; the very wrongest of forks. And the fork on the right was obviously the right fork.

Alyssa confidently picked up the fork on the right, avoiding the useless tool on the left. *Lord Jesus,* she prayed, *please always help me to pick the right fork.*

Fork in hand, she slammed the closet door and ran to find her siblings.

Mike was somewhat happy with the way things were working out. He took Dunwittee's alleged illness as an implied license to set up the Christmas service in any way he saw fit. And while it is certainly unusual to baptize on

Christmas Day, it would be entirely in keeping with both the purpose of the church and the meaning of the holiday.

He stopped Martin as the latter was getting into his car, a red Karman Ghia with a white racing stripe. Mike held the door open.

"Martin, something's come up for next Sunday. The pastor may be out ill. Would you be able to conduct the baptism?"

"Well, it's been a while, but I think I still remember all the words. And how badly could it go?"

"Mrs. Fenwick is going to lead the song service; she's found some songbooks that should get us out of the hymnals and still give us more of a guide than the projectors. Mrs. Henson's going to play the piano."

"Her playing has improved considerably of late, hasn't it? And her singing, also."

"I think that all she really needed was to feel that she was truly contributing to the church. Using her talents. So, after the music, we'll draw the curtains, you can say a few words about baptism, and then the baptism itself, and then we'll close them again."

"Do you think we should have something afterwards, you know, cookies and coffee or something, just to acknowledge the people who came for the baptism? There's always a bit of family that show up."

"Certainly cause for celebration."

"Then I thought we'd have special music; Mrs. Fenwick was planning to sing. That'll give Lupe time to help Emily get dried and dressed."

"Who's preaching?"

"Well, unless I can impose upon the Association Missionary, the two of us may have to do the rock-paper-scissors thing."

"What about Hiram?"

That stopped Mike cold. "Hiram? Mr. Cheebly?"

"Pastored 30-odd years, on and off, over in Los Lomas, before he retired. He was going deaf, and felt he was losing his edge, but still wanted to serve. So now he volunteers here as the janitor."

"I don't remember him ever preaching."

"He's been retired forever," said Martin. "And that church was always small, more of a mission, really. Most of his preaching was volunteer, or down at the mission on Soledad Street."

"I never knew that."

"He likes it that way."

"Should we give him a title? Pastor Emeritus?"

"He was of the opinion that a pastor should never seek honor and titles. Like that parable about going to a big feast, and sitting at the foot of the table, instead of the place of honor."

"My mind," said Mike, "Is well and truly blown."

As Mike made his way back into the auditorium, it occurred to him to see what other surprises might be in the closet. He retrieved the key, now so polished from use that it almost seemed to glow.

The closet opened almost at the first touch of the key, and there inside were seven candlesticks, all lighted and burning.

One of the candles had burned very low, and the wick smoked badly. The flame was very tiny, and the side of the candle had guttered, spilling its wax down the side, onto the shelf.

He was reminded of a time long ago, when, during a candlelight church service, a metal candle holder had gotten too hot, and had set fire to the tiny stub of wax that remained. What should have been an orderly and pretty flame had devolved into a burning ball of wax, smoking up the room and giving off a horrible smell.

At last a deacon had come with a cup of water, to quench the flame, and to remove the candlestick out of its place. The thought sent a chill into Mike's heart.

O Lord, our Lord, Who walks among the seven candlesticks, and holds the seven stars in His right hand, begged Mike, *please, for your Name's sake, do not remove our candle out of its place.*

---

1. *O Come, All Ye Faithful* is attributed to John Francis Wade, 1841.

2. *Angels We Have Heard on High* was translated from the French by James Chadwick in 1860. Its origins prior are shrouded in mystery.

Chapter Twelve

WARREN DUNWITTEE, OF NOCONA, Texas, was struck by conviction. Christ had implored the people to forgive their enemies, and to pray for those who had hurt them. And here he was, a practicing Christian – or so he said – who hated his brother.

Yes, Warren had to admit it. He hated him. He despised what Walter had become, and wished that the state of California would slide off into the ocean like Atlantis, so long as it took his brother along with it.

"It's not wrong to stop an injustice," said Warren, aloud, to the inside of his pickup truck.

It's wrong to hate the one who is unjust, came the reply, in his mind.

"I am not required to let my brother keep hurting me," he said. "I don't have to participate in his drama."

And at the same time, you cannot destroy him.

"But he's evil."

Vengeance is mine, saith the LORD, and I shall repay.

That was a Bible verse, from Deuteronomy. And the apostle Paul also used it in Romans, to dissuade Christians from seeking revenge. Warren could argue with his own thoughts and feelings, but not with scripture. He knew it in his heart, but his mind needed some convincing.

"Alright, I'll forgive him," said Warren, begrudgingly, at long last. "Is that what you want?"

He sat for a few minutes, trying to find the will to forgive his brother. He thought about Walter at their father's funeral, and the smug look on his face. He thought about Walter, in the very pulpit of their father's church, spewing blasphemy. It was like a slap to his father's face. Fire burned in Warren's heart.

"You really want me to forgive that?" He fumed for a moment. "How do I even know these thoughts in my head are from God?"

The Spirit convicts to correct; the accuser condemns to destroy.

Well, yes, this did seem to be about correcting things; about restoring his broken relationship with his brother. Thoughts started to come to Warren, thoughts not of war, but of peace, and of better times. He remembered playing marbles with Walter, in the small dirt yard behind the house. He remembered games of tag, under the spreading live oak, and searching for frogs together in the stream that ran alongside the ranch. He remembered the time they got into trouble for exploring the old Svengaard barn, or for breaking the rail fence by balancing on it.

He remembered dinners, chattering at the table until their mother told them to hush and to eat, while the food was still hot. He remembered praying at bedtime, and thanking God for his big brother.

Where did that all go wrong? A tear crept down Warren's cheek. He absently brushed it away.

"Lord God," he prayed, aloud, "I forgive Walter for all that he has ever done to me, and I ask you, O Holy Lord, to forgive him as well. If, on the last day, there are sins charged against his name, Dear God, hold him blameless for any sins against me."

He drew a gasping breath, wiping the tears from his eyes, and felt a great weight lift off of his shoulders; a weight he had never consciously felt until that second.

Right then, deep in his soul, he felt the grace of God, and in a flash it came to him, *Forgive us our debts, as we forgive our debtors.*

It took him several minutes to compose himself so that he could start the truck and drive himself home.

Wednesday Afternoon found Mike off of work, for once, and he decided to treat himself to a burger at Dorman's café. He was surprised to see Martin there, sitting with Luis and with Garth Fenwick. They waved him over, and pulled up another chair for him. The waitress appeared with a menu and put it on the table.

"Well, this is a surprise," he said. "What brings you fellows out?"

"I always eat here on Wednesdays," said Luis. "And these two were here already."

"I thought I'd invite Garth to lunch, and see how he's settling into Sardis," said Martin.

"And how do you find our little burg?" asked Mike.

"Quite well," said Garth. "The people have been very friendly, and the church seems like a great little congregation. I love the music program Mrs. Henson put on last week."

"The kids did very well," conceded Luis. "I didn't know they could sing in Latin."

"It was the best Christmas program in many years," said Mike. "I thought the kids were adorable."

Luis smiled and leaned back in his chair, obviously proud, even though only 60% of the children present had been his.

"So, I heard that pastor Dunwittee will be out on Christmas Sunday," said Garth.

"A bit of a cold, he thinks," said Mike. "We've asked a retired pastor from the area to speak tonight and on Christmas Day."

"Who's that?" asked Luis, raising an eyebrow.

"Hiram," said Mike.

"The Janitor?"

"He's a retired pastor, too," said Martin. "I think I remember him preaching a few times, long ago."

"Well, I guess for one week, it's okay," said Luis. "But my Emily, she's getting baptized!"

"Martin's going to do the actual baptism," said Mike. "It'll be fine."

"I hope so," sniffed Luis. "We're gonna have all the family there. It's not a good time for things to go wrong."

Mike thought of asking how a simple baptism could possibly go wrong, but he did remember a story once about a baptism candidate who was scared of being under water. She had flailed her legs in the air, and had gotten one knee hooked over the edge of the baptistry, so that it was difficult for the pastor to keep her head above water.

He thought of mentioning it, but Emily didn't strike him as a person who might panic. It would be fine.

"Emily is your older girl?" asked Garth.

"Thirteen," said Luis.

"The twins are nine. So far, we haven't talked to them about making a decision for Jesus."

"Sometimes it comes naturally," said Martin. "The Sunday School lessons and the music and the Bible stories. They just click, and the kids know that they need Jesus. Other times, they need an adult, or even a sibling, to sit down and talk it through with them."

"Faith and I have been struggling with that," said Garth. "We pray with them every night, but how do we know when they're ready?"

"Keep praying," said Mike. "God will have his hand on them. You'll feel it when they're ready."

The food came, and the men bowed their heads to pray before eating. Mike noticed that the waitress stood a few feet away, holding the coffee pot and waiting.

"You know, Fellows," said Mike, as they raised their heads after the prayer, "Perhaps we should make prayer lunches into a regular thing. Or a prayer breakfast of some kind. Whoever can make it, as informal as this right here."

The others nodded, and put their forks to good use.

That night, the service seemed to just fall into place, with no planning at all, so far as anyone was aware. Mrs. Henson led them in song, Martin led them in prayer for the Christmas Day service and baptism, and then Alyssa came forward and lit the purple candle.

"I see," said Hiram, as he came forward to the pulpit. "I see the light, and I see everything else because of the light. And who is the Light of the World?"

"Jesus," said Clarissa Fenwick, almost by accident. She hadn't meant to speak out loud. When she realized that everyone had heard her blurt it out, her eyes grew huge, and she looked at her mother, who merely smiled.

"That's right, young lady, and don't you ever be ashamed to say 'Jesus!' He is the light of the world!"

Clarissa looked at her sister, Marissa, and then back at the preacher again.

"I see the light," said Hiram. "And I see by the light. The Light of the world, Jesus, makes it so we can see. His light shines in the darkness, says John, and the darkness doesn't overcome it."

He paused and let them think about it.

"Now think about that. You go into a room that's filled with darkness, and you just carry that one candle. What's going to happen? Will the darkness, all that darkness, push out the light? Will the light be dimmed by that darkness? Will that candle start to flicker, like it might go out?

"No, no, it works the other way. That little bit of light cuts a tiny hole in the dark, and makes it yield. It pushes that darkness back. Because darkness is where the light is not; our darkness is where Jesus is not.

"Sin is like that darkness. It multiplies, and it fills up the whole room. But Jesus, Light of the world, gives us grace, and that grace pushes back against sin. It redeems. And the more we reflect that grace, the more we carry that candle into the darkness, the more that sin is broken, and pushed back, in Jesus' Name.

"I see that tonight we lit the Mary candle. Sunday, we're going to light the Christmas candle, the Jesus candle, because Jesus, the Light of the world, will be here. But tonight, we're talking about Mary.

"Some Christians put too much on Mary. Others of us, we maybe don't put enough on her. Mary was a good and godly woman, used of God in a unique way.

"Matthew tells us Mary's genealogy, and he mentions four other women. Anybody know who they were?"

"Ruth," said Mrs. Henson. "And Rahab."

"Two foreign women," said Hiram. "And one of them had a shady past. Who else?"

"Bathsheba," said Lupe.

"Tamar," said Faith.

"A lady whose King was up to no good, and a lady who, herself, got up to no good. All four of these women had something shameful in their past.

"And Matthew brings this around to Mary, because I'm sure there were people in her day who said things about her. She wasn't even fully married to Joseph, and here, she had a baby on the way. People must've thought some awful things about her."

Hiram shook his head for a moment.

"But that wasn't because of any sin. In fact, the Bible calls Mary a blessed woman, because through her, God gave us the greatest gift that has ever been given: A precious little baby boy who was God in the flesh.

"Now here's the thing: Some of us have got some shame in our pasts. You know what I mean. God's been talking to you, and you've been ignoring Him.

"Well, Jesus isn't here to expose your shame. He's not here to condemn you. John 3:17 says that He did not come to condemn the world, but that the World, through Him, might be saved.

"If you've got shame in your heart tonight, you come on up. You bring it to Jesus. You confess it to Him, and be healed of it. There's no better time than now."

Hiram walked around to the front of the pulpit.

"Maybe you don't have something shameful in your past, but you know that you need Jesus in your life. Now is the time. Don't wait."

Martin glanced across the room. Susan was there again, as she had been last Wednesday, and he watched with relief as she walked down the aisle to talk to Pastor Dunwittee. *Lord, please hear her prayer,* he prayed. *Son of David, have mercy; have mercy.*

Susan spoke to Hiram, and they bowed their heads together. After a few minutes, she turned and knelt at the altar. Hiram turned back to the people.

"Is there anyone else who needs to find Jesus? I cannot save you; I can only point you to Him, and He can save. Come now, don't wait."

Marissa whispered to Clarissa, who shook her head and whispered something back. There was a nearly-silent exchange of whispers, hisses, and facial expressions back and forth between the girls.

Just as Faith was about to tap them both on the head and give them a warning look, Marissa suddenly took Clarissa's hand. The two girls dashed up to Hiram and motioned for him to bend down. As he did, they started to whisper again.

Hiram, moving in the slow, careful way that old men do, sank to one knee, and listened to the girls. He prayed with them, then rose to his feet again, using the pulpit as a guide. He nodded to Faith, who quickly came to stand beside them.

"Folks, these two girls just told me that they want to follow Jesus. We prayed just now, and they asked Jesus to forgive their sins. What do you say about that?"

"Amen!" said Mike, just half a syllable ahead of the rest of the people. "Hallelujah!"

There was a closing song of praise; it may have been spontaneous. There was a prayer. And then there was a room full of happy Christians, joyful that two little girls had joined the family of God.

Chapter Thirteen

IN THE CLOSET, MRS. Henson found a hand bell. She smiled and swung it carefully from side to side. As she did, great huge church bells seemed to ring, sending the message far across the fields: *Christmas Day is here at last! Unto us, a Child is born! Unto us, a Son is given!*

She rang the bell long and loud, waking the sleepers far and wide. Then, holding the bell near her ear, she flicked it with her fingernail eight times.

Smiling from ear to ear, she put the little bell back into the closet and closed the door.

"Dear," said Luis, "Lupita, *mi Corazon*? Did you just hear a church bell?"

"Eight o'clock already? We are so late!" said Lupe, springing from bed. "Emily! Emily! Get up, quickly! We need to do your hair!"

Luis got out of bed. He didn't think that any of the local churches had a belfry, much less a bell. Still, he had heard what he heard.

He started down the stairs to begin breakfast. Towels were in the car, and dry clothes for Emily to change into.

Lupe had picked out a lovely white dress for her. There would be a reception in the church hall; the family would expect it. The cake was already there, placed in the church refrigerator the night before.

Luis would wear his best tie, and he had a smaller one for Efrem as well. It was time the boy learned how to tie a double Windsor.

It was a big day for the Cannon Family.

What ensued can best be called orderly chaos; each member of the family was in constant motion, eating, dressing, preparing, brushing, darting to and fro.

One moment stood out in Luis' mind, later: When he stood at the full length mirror, his son in front of him, as Luis reached around the boy and tied his tie. There was something oddly magical about that moment, something that filled him with deep joy.

He could never afterwards recall what it was that made the moment so great. All he had done was to explain how the squirrel ran twice around the tree before darting into the hole, and that thus ties were tied. Still, he found himself filled with pride.

For one fleeting moment, looking into the mirror, he saw Efrem and himself in the midst of a long chain of fathers and sons, passing down knowledge and approval from generation to generation. It was as if they had, in that moment, laid a foundation for a dozen generations after them, thereby fulfilling a solemn oath to a dozen generations before them.

And then Efrem was smoothing his hair, and darting to his room for the suit jacket that he would be expected to wear over the pale blue shirt and the navy tie.

At last they were all prepared, and they piled into the car, each scrambling for their proper place.

The scene at the Fenwick house was only slightly less chaotic. Faith spent far too long fussing about the girls' hair, and dressing them was twice as hard as usual, since they needed outfits for before and after the baptism.

And of course, there would be pictures taken, so everything had to be absolutely perfect. And did the girls remember the words to the song for the special music? Were they certain?

Garth, being a man of innate wisdom, carefully stayed out of the way, so as not to add any further stress to the morning.

Mike heard the bells, ringing across the plain, and tried to figure out from whence they came. The Catholics had nothing in their belfries; not even bats. There was an Anglican church over in Pergamum township, and a Presbyterian church in Laodicea, but surely he couldn't have heard them from Sardis.

He supposed that, regardless whose bells he had heard, he should get up early. The baptistry wouldn't fill itself, and he was a bit nervous, despite his assurances to Martin, that it might not be warm enough.

He found himself humming as he swung his feet out of bed, and it took him a moment to place the tune: It was *Joyful, Joyful, We Adore Thee,* and old hymn set to Beethoven's ninth symphony.

Laughing, he made his way to the shower.

George and Lucy Berklay awoke at the sound of the bells. It passed through George's mind that they hadn't been to church in forever, and it was Christmas Day, after all. He wondered what a service might be like at Mike's church. It might be a nice gesture, since Mike had gone out of his way to visit when Lucy's mother died.

But that thought was replaced by the realization that the bed was soft and warm, and that his dream had been pleasant and fulfilling. His legs felt as if they weighed tons, and were being pulled down into the mattress.

Lucy, in a groggy voice, softly asked, "Dya think we otta…" and then gave a soft snore. It inspired George, and he answered with a snore of his own. Soon they were both dreaming.

Susan heard the bells. She knew what they meant: She was being called back to God. Susan's orbit had taken her far from God, and she had shaped her life – well, her life after Martin – around making herself happy at all costs, and letting God tend to Himself.

God had called her back; He was calling her to church even now. But the thought terrified her. What had she meant, Wednesday night, giving her heart and her life to Jesus? It was as frightening now as when Martin had done it without talking to her about it.

What had she committed to? She knew the Bible; she knew the ways of God. The ways she had been living were not the ways of God. If she rebuilt her life around God, she'd have to start from scratch.

All the things she had put where God belonged … those would have to go. And that included the people that she had put before God. Relationships would need to end. Relationships that were working for her, that were filling a need in her life – she would need to give those up. Break them off. Let them go.

She shuddered at the thought of the pain she would need to endure, and the pain she would need to inflict. It wasn't going to be easy. But it was necessary.

A verse that the preacher had said to her came to her mind, that Jesus had despised the cross for the joy set before Him. She couldn't compete with that: The pain she would have to endure would be nothing like that, and in the end, it would be worth it, to be aligned with God once more. She knew that it had to happen.

Still, could she even do it?

Lord Jesus, she prayed, *Give me strength. Show me what to do. Help me to be who you want me to be. Help me tear down all my idols, until there is no one to worship but You.*

She couldn't go to church; she just couldn't. Not just now. Especially not on this most holy of days. Instead, she lay in her bed and wept.

---

1. *Joyful, Joyful, We Adore Thee* is a 1907 hymn by Henry Van Dyke, composed to be sung to Ludwig Von Beethoven's *Ode to Joy.*

Chapter Fourteen

THE FIVE CHILDREN ASSEMBLED on stage in two rows, with Efrem and Emily in the back. Alyssa and the two Fenwick children stood in front of them. Faith smiled at them, to remind them to smile at the church. The children each donned a painful smile, trying not to look directly at anyone in the pews.

Faith cleared her throat, a signal for Mike to start the tape. After a moment of hissing, the cassette yielded a catchy hammer dulcimer tune. Mike smiled. He'd always loved the Rich Mullins song, *Creed*. The words were merely a slight adjustment to the apostles' creed, with an original chorus by Mullins.

Faith waved her hands, and the children immediately chimed in. "I believe in God the Father," they sang, "Almighty Maker of heaven, and Maker of earth."

Given that it was being sung by children ranging in age from nine to thirteen, it sounded very nice. They followed the tempo, and were very nearly in tune, from beginning to end. Mike knew that he would be humming the tune to himself for the rest of the week.

He was so caught up in the special music that he almost missed the visitor. The man was very casually dressed in a tropical shirt and jeans, with fashionable running shoes on his feet. His hairstyle was a bit odd, but not outlandish, and he gave Mike the strong impression of being a foreigner.

He stood for a moment with his back to the door. It was as if he wasn't entirely sure what he had walked into, nor what he was expected to do next.

Mike quickly moved beside him and touched his arm, motioning towards a seat. The man muttered something that Mike didn't understand. When Mike asked him to repeat it, the man shook his head and said something that sounded like "Chess key." Then the man, understanding Mike's gesture, at least, slid into a vacant seat.

Unfortunately, there were a large number of vacant seats. Mike was grieved by the sparsity of the crowd. Or perhaps it was fortunate, since it gave the visitor a place to sit. Mike slipped back into the sound booth.

When the children were through singing, and their parents were through clapping, Faith gave them an emphatic nod. As the children scattered to their seats, Hiram strode up to the pulpit.

The advent candles were glowing brightly, with the large white Christ Candle, at the center, blazing with the brightest light. It made Mike think of John 1:5, "The Light shines in the darkness, and the darkness cannot overcome it." It was a glorious Sunday, a bright Christmas indeed. He smiled.

"So lovely to see these young folks taking a role in the church like this," he said. "God bless them. I understand that we'll be baptizing three of them later. So that makes it truly appropriate, this song that they sang today." He took a moment to shuffle the papers on the pulpit before continuing.

"You see, before Deacon Martin lowers each of these young people into the water, he's going to say, 'In whom do you place your faith and trust?' and they are expected to each answer, 'In Jesus Christ.'

"Baptism tells a story. It is a testimony to three things, and it is a sign of belief in the God who was, and is, and is to come. It is a testimony to belief in the Father, and the Son, and the Holy Spirit, in whose name, singular name, we will baptize them.

"Three persons, but we are commanded to baptize in the one name. If someone tells you that the Trinity is not in the Bible, you do like old Athanasius, and you punch that heretic in the nose.

"No, no, don't you do that. But anyone who tells you that the Trinity isn't in the Bible is a heretic. The Trinity is part and parcel of the Word of God. Can I get an amen?"

There were a few amens, mostly mumbled, though Mike's came through clearly. Hiram nodded. The visitor turned around and looked at Mike with a most puzzled look before turning back to the front.

"Now, like I said, these three young people are gonna demonstrate; they are going to act out for you, three important things. These are their messages to you.

"First, they are telling you that Jesus of Nazareth died, and was buried, and rose again on the third day."

Mike gave another amen, slightly more controlled, but Hiram didn't even pause.

"That's what being lowered into that water represents: it represents dying and going into the grave, like Jesus did. And being raised out of that water is a testimony that Jesus did not stay dead, but overcame sin and death for us forever.

"Some of you are thinking, now, Hiram, why are you preaching an Easter sermon at Christmas? Well, the fact is, without Christmas, there would be no Easter. When Jesus chose to lay aside His glory, and become a little baby, He knew that it meant being nailed on that cross some thirty-odd years later.

"But you turn now to Hebrews 12:2, and you read what He said about that cross. It says that He despised its shame. He did not just endure it, He didn't suffer through it, He despised it. He had contempt for it. It meant nothing in light of the purpose set before Him.

" 'Cross,' said He, 'Your terrors are naught to me. Hiram must be saved from the wages of his sin.' "

The visitor jumped slightly in his seat at that last sentence, as if startled.

"That's right, Jesus, the Baby born in a manger, the sinless Man who forgave the sinful, and taught them not to sin any more, died for me. For Hiram Cheebly.

"And He died for you. You were on His mind when He was on the cross. So He died, and was buried, and rose on the third day, and we are going to act that out, three times. Glory to God, Hallelujah, amen."

He paused for a moment and drew a deep breath.

"At the same time, these girls are telling you what's going on in their lives; that they are dying to sin, and burying their old ways in the grave with Jesus, and rising to walk a new life, a life with Jesus in control.

"Look with me in Romans 6:3, 'Or do you not also know that as many of us as have been baptized into Christ Jesus are baptized also into His death?' Now look down to verse 7, 'He who is dead is freed from sin.'

120

"These young ladies are telling us that they will not sit in the seat of the scoffer, nor walk in the ways of the wicked. Amen and amen. They are saying that Jesus is in control of their lives."

He paused again, and drew his breath slowly.

"Now the third message, that one's powerful as well. Because unless the Lord comes before then, each of these young ladies will one day lay in a real grave. But not forever. Oh, no. Not forever.

"The Lord Jesus will call them up out of that grave, just like He called for Lazarus, and just like Lazarus, they will rise up out of their graves.

"Hosea, prophet of old, said it in Hosea 13:14, and the Apostle Paul said it again in 1 Corinthians 15: 'Death, where is thy victory? Grave, where is thy sting?' Jesus, God incarnate, come to earth as a little baby, has beaten death and the grave, and He will call us forth."

Hiram stopped and stood still, drawing his mouth tightly closed; it was the only way to keep from weeping at the thought of Jesus' costly grace. He shook his head.

"Jesus paid it all," he said, at last, in a wavering voice. "All, to Him, I owe."

He closed his Bible and nodded to Faith. She motioned to the baptismal candidates, who got up and made their way to the rooms behind the platform, to prepare for Baptism.

The visitor got up and moved beside Mike. "Ty mluvíš česky?" he asked, with wide eyes. Mike shrugged and shook his head. The man moved back to his seat cautiously, as if he expected it to explode.

Mrs. Henson picked this moment to look around, and spotted the man sitting by himself. Well, a visitor sitting alone was not a thing to be permitted. She got up with a maternal grace and went over to sit beside him, as only an older lady can do.

Mike heard him whisper to Mrs. Henson, and saw her shake her head. "No," she said, in a stage whisper that Mike heard clearly. "The pastor only speaks English."

The visitor said something emphatic to Mrs. Henson, who shook her head and patted his arm. Her reply was lost to Mike, but the visitor looked around the room with saucer-sized eyes.

What could she have said that terrified him like that? But there was no time to wonder; the curtains were parting. Martin was already in the water, and the twins, holding hands and clutching the guide rails, cautiously made their way down the steps to stand beside him.

"Which of you is Clarissa?" Martin asked. One of the girls raised her hand. "Clarissa, in whom do you place your faith and trust?"

"In Jesus," she said, shyly.

Martin put one hand behind her back and the other in front of her chin, for her to cling to. "Clarissa Fenwick, upon your profession of faith, I baptize you now in the name of the Father, and of the Son, and of the Holy Spirit. Buried with Christ in baptism, rise to walk in the new life."

He quickly lowered her and then lifted her from the water. Martin repeated the ritual with Marissa. Then the two girls climbed up the steps from the baptistry, disappearing from view.

Moments later, Emily made her way down into the water, and the ritual was repeated once more. As Emily came up from the water, Lupe shouted "Amen!"

She hadn't meant to do it, and was as surprised as anyone. But she didn't feel the slightest bit embarrassed.

Hiram went to the podium again and started to lead in a chorus of *"What a friend we have in Jesus,"* but he was interrupted by the visitor, who darted up the aisle.

In talking about it later, Hiram was quite certain that the man asked, "What must I do to be saved?" and that Hiram answered, "Repent and believe on the Lord Jesus Christ." The man fell to his knees, dragging Hiram down with him. Hiram put a hand on his shoulder.

Uncertain what to do, the congregation continued a ragged rendition of the old hymn, slowly fading in volume and rhythm. Mike went up to the front, and faced the people. He cleared his throat.

"Let's continue with, *Shall We Gather at the River,*" he said, because it was one of the few songs with which he was comfortable as a song leader. The congregation followed, singing strongly now that they were being led.

As they reached the end of the verse, Hiram and the visitor stood up. "Folks," said Hiram, "This is Janek. He's from Prague, over in Europe, and today he's making a profession of faith, and presenting himself as a candidate for baptism. What is your pleasure?"

"Baptize him," said Mike. There was a chorus of amens, and there were a couple of hallelujahs. "Martin, get back in the water; there's one more."

Martin stuck his head around the corner of the baptistry window. "Huh?" he asked.

"There's one more to baptize. We'll send him back in a second. Man your battle station."

Martin shrugged and waded back down the steps.

The man began to speak, but in a foreign language. He gestured to Hiram, and then to Mike, and then to Mrs. Henson. He seemed to be on the verge of tears.

"I did not," said Hiram. "I said my own name."

"Oh," said Mrs. Henson, standing up in the back row. "He's speaking Czech. It all makes sense now. I thought he was speaking English." She said it in a very reasonable tone, as if she were saying that refreshments would be served.

Lupe looked sideways at Luis. Mrs. Henson spoke Czech? And couldn't tell it from English?

"He said that I said his name in the sermon," said Hiram. Janek replied in Czech.

"He says that he distinctly heard you say that Jesus despised the cross, because Janek must be saved."

"I said my own name, Hiram."

Mrs. Henson shrugged. "He heard Janek. And since he heard the entire sermon in Czech, I think we can assume that it wasn't your voice he heard, Hiram."

"Oh," said Hiram. His eyes got wide.

"Oh," said Mike.

"Yes," said Mrs. Henson.

Janek began to speak. She listened as Janek spoke, first with composure, but with tears slowly building in his eyes. "I hear you, Dear, and you're among friends," she said, when he stopped and wiped his face with his hands.

"Janek is a tourist from Prague," said Mrs. Henson. "He has been wrestling with what is truly important in life. There have been some problems in his personal life – a girlfriend, some family illness. And today – Well, today his thoughts were leading him down a very dark path.

"And then his car broke down. He managed to steer it into our parking lot, and he came in to see if he might borrow a phone. His own SIM card is only good in Europe. But Mike didn't understand him, when he asked about a phone. So he sat down, thinking that perhaps someone after the service might help him.

"And then he noticed that Hiram was speaking in Czech, or rather, that he was hearing Hiram's message in Czech. The Holy Spirit moved in his heart, and now he has chosen to follow Jesus.

"Here is water. It has been blessed for this purpose. What prevents him from being baptized?"

"Nothing at all," said Hiram.

The girls were coming back into the sanctuary, and were puzzled to see the men standing in the front, and Mrs. Henson speaking to everyone from the back row, but since they didn't know what to expect in a baptismal service, they just went to sit with their parents.

Mike led Janek around where the girls had just come, and pointed him to the baptistry. After a moment, he could be seen wading down into the water.

"Janek," said Martin, "In whom do you place your faith and trust?"

"Ježíš Kristus," he replied.

"Janek, upon your profession of faith, I baptize you now, my brother, in the Name of the Father and of the Son and of the Holy Spirit." He lowered Janek into the water.

There was a voice from a corner of the auditorium.

"Wait," he said, as Janek was raised from the water, a new creature.

Mike looked over to the newcomer. It was Pastor Dunwittee, and he was walking up the side aisle, loosening his tie.

"I need Jesus also. I was going to be anywhere but here, today. I was going to go camping at Mount Diablo, but it's closed. The entire mountain is closed today.

"So I came back here, and dressed for church, planning just to see it be a train wreck without me. But instead I find this – God is really here, he's really moving in our midst.

"I never believed that it was possible, just that the miracles were mere metaphors and parables. But this is like the day of Pentecost – people from other lands hearing the gospel in their own tongues. It's real. God's real. His Spirit is real.

"I've been such an idiot. I let the doctrines of men tear down my faith, and replace it with warm feelings and nice sayings. I made a god in my own image, instead of letting Jesus transform me into His.

"I see it; I get it. I've been trying to lead all of you to a new understanding of Christ, but what I needed was the old understanding of Christ. The understanding that all of you have had all along.

"Oh, Lord Jesus, forgive me. Father God, I am unworthy to be a son; make me only your servant.

"O Church, I have sinned against you. Please, show me the way to Jesus. Please, baptize me. I want – I want to follow Jesus. To follow the right way. As His servant."

Martin called out, as Janek made his way up and out of the water. "Come on, Pastor; there's room at the cross for everyone. Even preachers."

"Lord Jesus, forgive me," Dunwittee cried out. Mike walked over and embraced him, then led him behind the wall, towards the baptistry.

"Your sins are surely forgiven," said Hiram, "In the Name of Jesus, standing upon His Word, 'Whosoever calls upon the name of the Lord shall be saved.' "

"Pastor," said Martin, but the Dunwittee immediately stopped him.

"Call me Walter," he said. "I haven't truly been a pastor to this church."

"Very well. Walter Dunwittee, in whom do you place your faith and trust?"

"In Jesus Christ," said Dunwittee. "Not as a myth, not as an ideal, but as the one true and living God, as He alone knows Himself to be."

"Amen," shouted Hiram.

Reciting the formula once more, Martin lowered Dunwittee under the water, and the water cascading from Walter's face hid the tears that streamed down his cheeks.

The service did not end immediately. Faith led them in a chorus, and then another, and finally Hiram led them in a long prayer.

When it was through, they all retired to the fellowship hall. A luncheon, and a cake, had been prepared to celebrate the girls' baptism, but in true Baptist fashion there was more than enough food for everyone.

When everyone had eaten their fill, and enough photos taken for a high school yearbook, Mike found Hiram sitting with Janek, casually chatting about the day of Pentecost. He couldn't help wondering how much each understood of the others conversation, but since they were both clearly engaged in it, he didn't ask.

"Hiram," he said, "I'm sorry to interrupt, but we need to step into the office for a moment. I need to cut the honorarium check."

"Now, you don't need to pay me," said Hiram. "That service today was a blessing from God, and you want me to take money for it?"

"If you don't, it will mess up our bookkeeping," said Mike. This was not a lie; the books were that fragile, and it was all that Mike could do to keep them untangled. But Mike was mainly motivated by the verse from Proverbs 3, *"Do not withhold good from them to whom it is due, when it is within your power to do so."* There was also a verse about not muzzling the oxen that treads the grain, but Mike was a bit uncertain of the propriety of comparing an ordained man of God to an ox, however large the preacher might be. In a pinch he might justify ministerial largesse by saying that the workman is worthy of his hire, but he could never remember that it came from Luke 10:7, so he refrained from saying it.

A brief disagreement followed, but Mike finally prevailed through sheer persistence. The two men make their excuses and threaded their way to the office.

In the office, the journal was lying on the desk. Mike had last seen it on the top shelf, so how it got to the desk was a mystery, but he saw no need to remark on it. Hiram picked it up.

"Well, I'll be," he said, as he opened it. "Where ever did this come from?"

"We found that in a closet," said Mike. "Up behind the baptistry."

"Do you know what this is?"

"A journal from a frustrated pastor," said Mike. "But I've found some real insight in it."

He slid the check across the desk to Hiram.

"That's too much," said Hiram.

"It's the normal honorarium," insisted Mike.

Hiram sighed. "Well, alright. But I'm accepting this under protest, so you know." He tapped on the leather cover of the journal. "This belonged to my father, back when he was pastor at the church in West Chualar. He went through some hard times out there, and those folks gave him a rough go of it.

"But in the end, it worked out well. While I was off in Bible college, there was a revival, and last I heard, that church is doing very well."

"You should publish this," said Mike, holding it out to Hiram. "I've gotten a lot of good from it."

"Then you keep it," said Hiram. "I'm too old for it to be of use to me, and I've got no one to give it to. You want to publish it, you do that."

"I'd be honored," said Mike.

By the time the men returned, Janek was nowhere to be seen. Dunwittee was talking with Luis. All of the tables had been put away, and the floor swept. Only the two men remained.

"Where's Janek?" asked Hiram.

"He tried his car again, and it's running fine," said Luis. "A couple of us went out to see if we could help, and it started on the first go."

"Well," said Hiram, "That was a God thing."

---

1. *Jesus paid it all; all to Him I owe,* is from an 1865 hymn by Elvina Hall.

2. *What a Friend We Have in Jesus* is an 1855 hymn by Joseph M. Scriven.

3. *Shall We Gather at the River* is an 1864 hymn by Robert Lowry.

Chapter Fifteen

MIKE CAREFULLY SCHEDULED HIS lunch hour, and made it to the Wednesday Men's' Prayer Lunch only a few minutes late. Martin had graciously ordered for him, so a clear soft drink sat at his place when he arrived.

Garth was asking for opinions on the beatitudes, and in particular what it meant to be "Poor in Spirit." Janek was doing his best to follow the conversation, using a phrasebook and a translation app on his phone.

George shook Mike's hand as Mike sat down. With his retirement coming through, George would be able to attend these lunches on a regular basis. At the moment, the Bible discussion sounded like Greek to him, but the men were friendly, and he enjoyed the fellowship.

Luis was there, and one might have thought that the regular lunches were his idea, from the proud look on his face. To be honest, he was as glad as George to have the fellowship, even if the discussion was perhaps a bit more churchy than those to which he was accustomed.

Still, he found himself liking Garth. And he was also pleased with the new direction in which the church was headed, though for the life of him, he really couldn't quite explain what about it pleased him. Perhaps it was simply that there was a different feel to it; more of a kinship, and less of a formality.

"How's Susan doing?" asked Mike, discreetly, into Martin's ear.

"One day at a time. She's dealing with a lot of issues. It's not easy seeing herself as someone God actually loves. She's been down some rough roads. Keep praying."

"Will do," he said, as Luis made a remark to Garth about a poverty of spirit perhaps meaning not acting like one is rich and powerful.

Garth nodded, and then replied that it might be deeper than that. The men batted the phrase around the table, with several of them offering a thought or two.

"I understand that the new tire plant is stirring up some trouble down at city hall," said Martin.

"Not exactly," said Garth. "But there's a deal going through with the City of Smyrna. Sardis isn't big enough or organized enough to provide a fire brigade if there were a problem at the plant."

"So we'd be paying Smyrna to cover the tire plant?" asked Luis, making a face. Clearly, the idea of higher city taxes did not appeal to him.

"Well, another proposal is to allow Smyrna to annex Sardis. Sardis would be known as West Smyrna."

"Would that benefit Sardis?"

"Indirectly, yes. Better tax base for the roads and the schools. Plus Smyrna will have to agree to a revitalization project for the Sardis old town."

"What does Smyrna get out of it?" asked Mike.

"Well, that puts the tire plant in Smyrna, technically, so they can claim to have added new jobs. And claim to be a growing town, as well. Things like that attract new people to the community."

"Sounds kind of synergistic," said Luis, nodding his head. Janek couldn't find the word in his phrasebook, so there was some whispering while Martin explained the idea to him.

"Fr'en's," said Janek, "Zitra, tomorrow, I am go, I vracim do Prahy, yes? Please, what word? Please modlete se za mě." He placed his hands together, palm to palm, fingers upward.

"Pray," said Mike. We will pray for you, yes."

"My family? My rodina. I say for them."

"You'll be telling them about Jesus," said Mike. "Yes, we will pray. We will pray often for you."

"Prosim, děkuji vám, přátelé."

"In fact," said Martin, "Let's start now."

As the waiter began to slide plates of food in front of them, Martin led the group in a short prayer for Janek's family; that they would all be open and receptive to the gospel message.

Janek closed his eyes, a vain attempt to stop the tears forming there. "Děkuji vám, přátelé," he repeated.

"It is our pleasure, brother Janek," said Garth, as the men turned their attention to their meals.

Former Pastor Dunwittee was packing. Most of his things would go into storage, to leave the parsonage available for the new pastor of the newly-renamed West Smyrna Baptist Church.

The word "parsonage" might have been excessively grand for the humble cottage. It consisted on a two-bedroom bungalow set on a small plot down the street from the church. One of the fences, just outside Dunwittee's bedroom window, was shared with an auto parts store parking lot. The opposite fence was shared with a utility yard of some sort, with bizarre machinery allegedly used for the municipal water supply.

Behind the parsonage, a steep hillside dropped down into a ravine dug long ago, against flooding that the dry town had never experienced. Dunwittee wondered if it was a precaution, or merely wishful thinking on the part of city planners.

It didn't matter. Dunwittee would be moving back to Texas. He hadn't really picked out a specific town, or even lined up employment. He doubted that there were many jobs for folks like him, trained in a liberal theology that they no longer believed. Still, it was better than the way things had been, here at Sardis.

It wouldn't be easy to face his brother. That barb, "Got kicked out of that church in California?" still stung.

Technically, he had kicked himself out of the church. His resignation was on the desk in the office, with a large note on it addressed to Mike.

It hadn't been easy to admit that Mike was right and that he was wrong. But it was the truth, the objective truth, and Dunwittee was finding that knowing and speaking the truth was worth any price he might have to pay. Even if it meant eating crow.

Well, he would need to go and eat crow in Texas. He was sure that Warren wouldn't let him off easily.

A blue two-tone Ford pickup, a relic from the 1970s, eased into his driveway. It was clean and well-polished, with large mirrors that stuck out from each side like a child with huge ears.

The truck eased to a stop behind Dunwittee's car, a modest Toyota Corolla, from the 1990s.

At first Dunwittee wondered if Mike had come to see him off, or possibly to gloat a little. No, that couldn't be. Mike wasn't like that. Dunwittee would have been, until last Sunday's service. But Mike never had been, and never would be.

Putting down a box of books – useless books, he now realized, books best given away, or used to level tables – he walked out to see who had come.

Warren took his time getting his footing as he emerged from the truck. Not his physical footing, but his mental and verbal footing. There was an apology to be made, and as his father would have said, "Sooner begun, sooner done."

Walter caught sight of him and moved quickly towards him. Warren swallowed, expected harsh words.

"Now, Walter," he said, but no other words came. Walter threw his arms around Warren and pulled him close, in a brotherly hug.

"Warren. You came all this way."

"Well, how could I not come?" he asked, untangling himself from his brother's embrace. "We're brothers, after all, and you sounded like you weren't alright." He took a step back. "That's still no cause to be hugging people."

"You were right, and I was wrong," said Walter.

"About what?"

"About everything. About God, about Dad, about what to do with my life." Walter shrugged. "Go ahead: You can tell me what a fool I've been, and how Dad would be ashamed."

"Well, honestly, Dad would be ashamed of me," said Warren. "I was very harsh with you, and I had no cause. I was very angry, and I have been since you came home from college, all those years ago."

"I'm sorry for that," said Walter. "I know I hurt you and Dad deeply."

"Well, this is no place to be doing our sorries," said Warren. "Out here in the public street, in front of God and everybody."

"There's no wrong place to apologize."

"If we have to do this, I'm sorry, too. And I forgive you for everything. Hope you'll forgive me."

"Without a doubt," said Walter. "Come on in and have some tea."

"Are we talking real tea, or that horrible chamomile stuff that you drink?"

Walter laughed, and for some reason, this made Warren laugh, and the two reconciled brothers found that they couldn't stop laughing.

Emily could no longer find the key, or the door into which it fit. In time, she came to wonder if it had been real. She was certain, beyond any doubt, that her parents had turned some sort of a corner that year, and had somehow renewed their marriage; whether a ring and a scroll found in a closet had been parts of the cause, well, that seemed more like a dream.

She was also certain that something had happened to the church, something that had revitalized it. Under the guidance of the Fenwicks, the music ministry blossomed, and soon incorporated a youth choir. She had many fond memories of that youth group.

The church bloomed as well, and the next pastor was a man wholly devoted to God. His sermons struck people in the heart, and many lives began to be changed. She remembered seeing friends walk the aisle, as she had, and she remembered happily cheering at their baptisms.

In time, some of the older folks went on to Glory, such as Old Mrs. Henson. Emily cried at her funeral, even though she knew that Mrs. Henson was now teaching piano to the angels. But she smiled when she thought of the legacy Mrs. Henson had left behind, in the life of the church, and of the Cannon children. Emily would always think of her as a kind of a third grandmother.

Seven years after the First Baptist Church of Sardis became the West Smyrna Baptist Church, Emily once again remembered the key. It was at the rehearsal dinner for her wedding, and in an odd conversational twist, she started to tell her intended groom all about the very odd dreams she had had as a child, concerning that quaint old church, in which she had grown up.

Alyssa, the maid of honor, listening intently, leaned across the table and said, "Remember when we put that old diadem on Mrs. Henson's head?"

Efrem, a groomsman, sitting beside Alyssa, laughed out loud. "She started singing like the choirs of heaven," he snorted. "And remember that big huge sword we found in the closet?"

Emily stared at them, mouth agape. How could they remember her odd dreams? Had she told them about them? She must have.

From that moment, there was lively debate about whether the key and the closet had been real, or just some childhood fantasy game that they had made up.

When the evening's formalities were done, the four of them – the Cannon children and a quite puzzled young man named Kurt – went down to the church to see the closet for themselves.

They persuaded Old Deacon Mike to meet them there and to let them in. At first he had refused, but when they explained why they needed into the church, he laughed and said that he'd be there directly.

Mike opened the church and turned off the alarm, as the four young people darted off to their adventure. For the Cannons, it was a delightful taste of nostalgia. Kurt was wondering what sort of madness ran in this family that he was marrying into, but it seemed harmless enough.

The shelf was there, in the children's wing, but there was no key upon it. They found the room into which the closet had opened, but there was no door, nor any sign that there had ever been a door. They searched adjacent rooms, and baffled poor Kurt with long, rambling tales, punctuated with gales of laughter, about the various things that had been found in the closet.

Efrem chasing Emily down the side aisle: It was a miracle he hadn't accidentally beheaded her. The story of the diadem, and the sword drills, and the curious old lantern, like the kind you find in train museums: They left nothing out, and it became clear to Emily that those dreams were never merely dreams.

Kurt, being good-natured, took it as some sort of childhood game, and the romp about the church as the turning of a page. The next day, they would be there again, and with an oath, the world would change; this moment, this last silly caper, this escapade, was, to his wonderful bride, a sort of a farewell to childish things. He could not help but lovingly indulge her.

When questioned later, Mike denied that there had been any sort of building renovations or remodeling up there behind the baptistry. When asked if he remembered the closet, and the things that came out of it, Mike would only laugh.

In all the days from then until now, neither the key nor the door was ever found again.